BRENDA HILL

lives in Southern California and is currently working on her next novel. She enjoys hearing from her readers. You can send an email from her website, brendahill.com.

BRENDA HILL
WITH FULL MALICE

WORLDWIDE®

TORONTO • NEW YORK • LONDON
AMSTERDAM • PARIS • SYDNEY • HAMBURG
STOCKHOLM • ATHENS • TOKYO • MILAN
MADRID • WARSAW • BUDAPEST • AUCKLAND

Recycling programs
for this product may
not exist in your area.

ISBN-13: 978-0-373-18968-7

With Full Malice

Copyright © 2012 by Brenda Hill

A Worldwide Library Suspense/February 2015

First published by Five Star Publishing

www.Harlequin.com

Printed in U.S.A.

WITH
FULL
MALICE

Acknowledgments

To the following, I extend my deep appreciation for sharing your time and expertise. Thank you.

To Robert Dearmore, Sergeant (Ret.) Los Angeles County Sheriff's Department, and his patient wife, Sheila; D. J. (Don) Stephens, nearly ten years military service, Airborne Ranger, Sniper and Small Arms; Claire Marie Teeters, Editor, *Yucaipa/Calimesa News Mirror*; Debi Faris, Founder, Garden of Angels Safe Surrender for Newborns; the staff of Desert Lawn Memorial Park & Funeral Home, Calimesa, CA; the paramedics and EMTs in Calimesa and Yucaipa, CA, who allowed me to interrupt their off time to ask questions; Wayne Hall, Legal Dept., Denny's Corporation, Spartanburg, SC; Patti Wollerton, General Manager, Denny's, in Yucaipa, CA, and her wonderful staff; Southwest Airlines Customer Relations; Yuma Community Food Bank, Yuma, AZ; Chelle Cordero, Stony Point Ambulance Corps, New York State Emergency Medical Technician; Brandon G. Cole, D.C., and his wife, Rosa Cole; Diane Mierzwik, Yucaipa Writers' Gallery; John McLeod, Yucaipa; Carolynn & Catie and the crew, Postal Annex, Yucaipa. And to Maxine Piotrowski. Thanks, everyone. All the errors are mine.

To our wonderful law enforcement officers in Yucaipa. You've worked hard to keep our community safe. Thank you.

To First Readers Ginny Lewon, Joyce Hunt, Earl C. Baker, Cheryl McDaniel.

To authors M. Jean Pike, Victoria Howard, Michael Prescott.

To my patient editor, Alice Duncan. And to Tracey L. Matthews, Content Project Editor, Five Star, and to Tiffany Schofield, Acquisitions Editor, Five Star. You're the best!

And always, my love and thanks to Roger & Debbie Bowman, who dropped everything countless times to respond to my SOS calls. And to Amanda, Kyle and Sean, the lights in my life.

ONE

IF THAT SCUMBAG deserved anything, it was to die.

She had planned it to the smallest detail, but anything could go wrong. If her timing was off a split second, if a customer appeared at the wrong time, if, if, if. She had to do everything she could to make sure nothing unexpected happened.

She turned into the restaurant parking lot, pleased to note only two vehicles besides his. If her luck held, the steakhouse would stay dead for another fifteen minutes or so.

Jeff Hawley's rusty red pickup faced south, with the driver's door opposite the restaurant's windows.

It couldn't have been better.

"All systems go," she murmured, using dialogue from an old movie she'd recently watched.

She had chosen a dark blue Chevy Aveo that at dusk might appear blue, dark green, or black. After leaving the rental agency, she'd taken Sand Canyon Road over the hill from Yucaipa to the orange groves and had smudged dirt on the California plates.

At the steakhouse, she parked so she could keep watch on the front door. Hawley was inside, enjoying his dinner. If she were successful, it would be the last thing he'd enjoy.

She placed the wide-brimmed straw hat on her head, dug in the shopper's tote for the surgical gloves and tugged them on, then retrieved the oversized man's long-sleeved shirt and draped it over her blouse. She checked the washcloth in the plastic bag. Good. It still had enough moisture to wipe away any splattered blood.

Next came the gun. She snapped the case open and lifted the black Glock 26 9mm from its egg-crate-foam bed. She screwed the titanium silencer onto the threaded barrel, but before loading the magazine, she paused. Did she really want the extra weight and length of a silencer on the gun? How would she be able to conceal it when she approached Hawley?

She glanced around the parking lot. Still dead, so deciding to take her chances, she unscrewed the silencer and loaded the magazine containing hollow-point bullets.

Even though the G26 was a powerful subcompact, it felt good in her hand. From the back of the slide to the tip of the barrel, it was about six inches long. Loaded, it was heavier than the small-caliber revolvers she'd fired as a teenager when target shooting in Wyoming with her father, but last week she'd ventured into the woods for some practice just to get the feel of the gun. The low bore axis design helped reduce muzzle rise in recoil, so hitting him quickly in the targeted areas should be no problem.

Once more she went over the plan: he'd leave through the front door, and she would approach him as he walked to his pickup. Then, if her luck held, he'd turn his back to her and she would have the perfect excuse to trail after him.

Then she'd nail him.

It sounded simple enough, but the timing was critical. She had to shoot after he passed the restaurant windows and just before he entered his pickup. And she would have to fire before he saw the gun. If he overpowered her and called the cops, they'd come, even for him. Then what would she do?

She couldn't allow that to happen.

She picked up the engraved envelope she'd received in

the mail. Inside, a note-sized sheet of paper had today's date stamped below an elaborately scripted header, The Ruby Red Society. There was no signature or return address. She folded the note and slid it back into its envelope to dispose of along with the tote.

Beads of sweat rolled under her bra. Sweat slicked her hands. No matter how determined she was to kill him, she felt moments of doubt.

Was she doing the right thing?

She had gone over her decision many times, debating first one issue then the other, but she always reached the same conclusion.

He had to die.

Behind her, rush-hour traffic on Yucaipa Boulevard was thinning out. To the west, the amber sun slid behind the San Bernardino Mountains, and the first stars sparkled in the coral-and-indigo sky.

She went over the plan once more, making sure she remembered every step. Did she have it down? Would she make some simple mistake like forgetting to pick up the casings?

The straw hat scratched her tender scalp. She squirmed in her seat. What on earth was he doing? He'd had time to eat three meals.

A minivan pulled into the lot and headed for a parking spot by the restaurant door.

No, no, no! She didn't want witnesses! Maybe, if he stayed inside for a while longer, it would be okay. Tracking the car's progress, she caught a glimpse of children in the backseat.

She went cold. Not children. She might chance adult witnesses if other circumstances were right, but she'd scrap the plan before risking trauma to a child.

She checked the restaurant door.

"Not now," she whispered, "don't leave now."

The minivan doors slid open and two boys around twelve years of age jumped out. A man and woman followed, both dressed in jeans and gold T-shirts with large blue numbers on the back.

Hurry inside, she urged. Hurry!

Only when they had made it safely inside did she breathe. Immediately after, the door swung open again and Hawley stepped out. His lean figure passed the restaurant windows and she tightened her grip on the gun. She scanned the lot behind to make sure no one was pulling in.

This was it.

Now! Go now!

She grabbed the shopper's tote and slipped out of the car. Sliding the gun inside her pocket, she headed straight for him.

Hawley shuffled toward his pickup with his shoulders hunched and head down as if he didn't want anyone to notice him. She hoped he was ashamed, but he probably wasn't. His type seldom was.

Just as she got within ten feet of him, he raised his head and looked directly at her. For just a second, she was taken aback by his handsome face, the green eyes, slim nose, full mouth. No one would have guessed how rotten he was inside simply by looking at him.

Like Satan, she thought. Beautiful on the outside.

She flashed her winning smile and tried to look helpless. "Excuse me, could you help me? I'm so scatterbrained that I've lost my—"

"Go away," he mumbled, brushing by her.

Perfect, she thought, trailing slightly behind. Just ignore me, keep your back to me.

Suddenly, as though alerted something was wrong, he

began to walk faster toward the red pickup and reached for the driver's door handle.

Now!

So fast it was almost one movement, she dropped the tote, pulled out the gun, and lifted it with both hands. He must have heard the tote hit the ground, because he spun around and saw the gun.

"No!"

She aimed for his heart and pulled the trigger. Blood sprayed from a blackened hole in his shirt and he staggered backward. The pistol recoiled, but she stepped forward and fired a second time, knocking him off his feet. Bending over his sprawled form, she fired again, putting a round through his temple. Blood splattered, chunks of skull flew, and he was still.

From behind her, someone shouted and she heard footsteps pounding toward them. She dropped the gun into the tote, snatched the warm casings from the pavement and pulled off the gloves, dropping them all into the tote. A man about thirty, wearing a baseball cap, pushed her down beside the pickup.

"What happened?" Crouching beside her, he glanced wildly in all directions.

"He's dead, he's dead!" she screamed. "Somebody killed him!" Staring in horror at Hawley's body, she rose.

"Get down!" He tugged her arm to pull her back down, but she didn't budge.

"Are you hit? Did you see who shot him?"

"A man…shot him and ran…" She dropped her voice to a whisper as if she were going into shock.

"Which direction?"

She simply stared at him.

"Which way did he go?"

She blinked several times before pointing to the empty field next to the restaurant.

"He must be gone." He patted his shirt pocket. "Damn, must've left my cell phone inside. You got one?"

She forced herself to remain expressionless.

"It's okay," he told her in a soothing voice. "My wife will call the cops. Just please, lady, get down and stay down until they get here." Crouching, he crab-walked to the victim. "Who is he?"

When she said nothing, he turned his attention to Hawley. Crossing himself, he began CPR. Only then did she ease back a few steps.

Confident it was too late to save the dirtbag, she turned and, carefully pacing her steps, headed for the Chevy. Just walk. Don't draw attention to yourself.

A woman behind her screamed and someone shouted something about an ambulance, but she didn't look back. Keeping her measured pace as she approached the car, she yanked off her hat and oversized shirt and stuffed them into the tote. Then she wiped her blood-splattered face and neck with the rag and dropped it with the other things.

It wasn't until she reached her car that she risked a quick glance backward. Several people were gathering around the pickup. Pole-mounted floodlights flipped on, illuminating the entire parking lot.

Time for her escape, but she didn't have to rush.

No one suspected her; no one was even looking her way. Even if someone saw her, her feigned innocence shone brightly, like a golden halo.

Now all she had to do was unload the tote and she'd be home free.

TWO

HE LAY FACEUP on the pavement outside of Jimmy's Steakhouse, arms and legs spread. Like a snow angel, Madison thought, only this angel had chunks of his skull blown away.

Blood pooled around his head and torso, staining his plaid shirt, the pavement, and splattering the pickup beside the body. Madison caught a glimpse before the medics surrounded him and hoped she wouldn't disgrace herself by passing out.

Revolving lights from the fire truck and two San Bernardino County Sheriff's Department patrol cars threw a kaleidoscope of reds and blues on the restaurant and the gathering crowd. Sirens wailed in the distance, growing louder as more teams responded to the *Shots Fired* alert.

"Grab the BVM!" A female paramedic bent over the victim. An EMT slapped a ventilator mask into her hands. "Start compressions!"

No matter how they tried to resuscitate, Madison doubted anyone could live after such a massive head wound. What were his last thoughts? she wondered. Had he known he was going to die?

"Miss! Miss!" a deputy shouted, pushing her back with the gathering crowd. "Please step back."

She stumbled back about ten feet, and with trembling hands, retrieved her camera from the briefcase slung over her shoulder. She took deep breaths as her therapist had taught her and snapped photos of the scene, trying to maintain a professional demeanor, wishing she were anywhere but here. This was her first crime scene as a reporter, and it was certainly going to be her last.

An ambulance pulled into the parking lot, followed by several other vehicles. Cutting its siren and flashing lights, it cruised toward the victim, the crowd parting to make a path as if they were a living Red Sea. The crew unloaded a gurney and pushed it toward the victim.

Madison stepped to the side and punched Marie's number on her cell phone.

"Where are you?" She tried to keep her voice below a shriek. "What's taking so long?"

"Traffic snarl on the 605," Marie Campbell, the *Yucaipa Tribune*'s editor told her. "Sorry to do this to you, kid, but it looks like it'll be at least an hour before I can get there. Talk to witnesses and hang in there. You're doing good."

"Yeah, sure," Madison said to a dead line. She wished she'd never called Marie in the first place. Of all the times she could have picked to do a review of the steakhouse, it had to have been that night. And of course it was one of those rare nights when not one of the three news reporters was available.

If she ever saw emergency lights at a review site again, she'd simply turn her car around and leave.

A collective moan came from the gathering crowd and Madison moved to get a better view. The EMTs had halted their efforts and were gazing at the navy-clad paramedic.

"Call it," she said, rising and pulling off her latex gloves.

An EMT disconnected monitor leads, while another pulled an IV tube from the needle. A deputy stepped forward, glanced at the body, then spoke into the microphone on his shoulder. Another deputy began cordoning off the immediate area with yellow tape.

He's dead, Madison thought, staring at the victim before

they covered him with a tarp. She hadn't known him, but she felt like weeping.

A deputy took notes from the paramedics, and a few moments later, the fire truck's diesel engine revved up several degrees to a loud clatter. When it pulled out, followed by the ambulance, most of the waiting crowd broke up and headed for their cars.

What now? Madison wondered. Talk to witnesses, Marie had said. Oh, Lord, she didn't have any training as a reporter and didn't want any. Her nice, safe, restaurant review job was just right for her, as far away from violence as she could get.

But Marie was depending on her, so she turned her camera to a sheriff's patrol car, its front doors open, splitting the black-and-gold logo along the side. A deputy sat inside, writing on a clipboard and talking to a man in civilian clothes. A witness, Madison thought, wondering if she should approach him, what she'd ask if she got the opportunity, all the while praying Marie would hurry up and get there so she could go home to her quiet apartment and well-ordered life.

About six feet from the open patrol car, another deputy stood talking to a young family who looked as if they'd just come from a Little League game. She hoped, for the kids' sake, they hadn't seen the shooting.

Madison exchanged her camera for her notebook and thought of the mantra she'd overheard from the reporters: Get the five Ws: who, what, when, where, why, and how. Okay, six.

She jotted down her impressions of the victim. Late thirties, perhaps. Shorter than her ex-husband, so probably around five-nine or less. Hair color? Difficult to tell with all that blood. His eyes? She'd never forget how they looked, half open and staring, as if accusing his tormentor—or begging for his life as she imagined her parents had done.

"You from the paper?" the fortyish man standing next to her asked. "Can't believe this. Me and the wife here"—he tugged the arm of a straggly haired blonde next to him—"just stopped to have a bite."

Determined to stay focused, Madison flipped to a new page. "Did you see what happened?" she asked, then remembered to ask their names.

"Middleton," he told her. "That's M-I-D-D-L-E-T-O-N." He paused long enough to make sure she got it, then recited his phone number. "Me and Candy got here just ahead of the fire truck, but that guy saw it all," he added, jerking his head toward the sheriff's car. "He was there."

"Did you talk to him?"

"Nah, he was doing that CPR-thing until the medics took over, but I heard him talking to the cops."

Although Madison avoided looking at the body, she was aware of him lying there, covered in his own blood. Had he known they were trying to save him? Had her parents known? Her legs wobbled. Locking her knees, she tried to concentrate.

"Did he see who did the shooting?"

"I don't think so, but the woman with him might know something."

"What woman? Where? With the witness or the victim?"

Middleton shrugged. "Wasn't no woman when me and Candy got here, but that's what he said. Older woman, he told them. Before I could hear anything else, the cops pulled him to the car."

"Older? How old?"

"I don't know. Old."

Madison added *senior woman* to her notes.

Just then two more patrol cars arrived and a county CSI van pulled into the site. Doors flew open and the crew unloaded boxes of lights and equipment.

Madison imagined them finding a chunk of bloody skull and all her reserve crumbled. The ground swayed.

"Lady, you all right?" Middleton grabbed her arm.

"Maddy!" a male voice boomed from several feet away.

No one but her grandmother and San Bernardino County Homicide Detective Dexter Quinn called her by that name. She tolerated it from Grandma Ella, and under different circumstances, she would've berated Dexter for it, but now his voice was the most beautiful sound she had ever heard.

"Dex."

He was standing behind the tape, a notepad in hand, talking to a deputy. At six-four, his white hair in the same flattop he'd worn as a college football player thirty years ago, he was a mountain of a man. How had she missed his arrival?

Sliding his notebook into his pocket, he strode toward her, his linebacker's bulk expertly cutting through the crowd. She felt the strength of his supporting arms, and his familiar scent of soap and aftershave offered a safe haven.

"Can you walk?"

Head down, she nodded, too embarrassed by her weakness to show her face. Dexter kept an arm around her and led her to his Tahoe.

She should have protested, should have questioned more people, but her wobbly knees desperately needed a moment's rest. Besides, few people argued with Dexter Quinn. Once again he was rescuing her, just as he'd done when she was six.

He helped her into his eleven-year-old SUV and retrieved a bottle of water from the rear floorboard. She took a long drink and leaned her head against the soft gray leather. She sighed. Safe again.

Her teeth began to chatter.

Dexter must have noticed because he snatched a fuzzy blanket from the backseat and spread it over her.

"You could use a shot of whiskey. Got anything stronger than iced tea at home?"

"Diet cola," she said, attempting a joke. The warmth from the blanket was seeping into her bones.

"You look like hell," he said. "What in God's name are you doing here? Of all the people I know, you shouldn't be at a crime scene."

"Marie—"

"You're not bucking for a reporter's job, are you? That would be the worst mismatch since your sorry attempt at marriage."

"You're incorrigible, but I love you anyway." Keeping a watchful eye for Marie, she explained why she was there. "I wonder who he is…was."

"Hey, listen to me. Don't worry about him, you hear? There's nothing you can do for the guy now, and it's you I'm concerned about."

"I'm a big girl now."

"Take a look at your face and tell me how big you are. You still look as if you're going to pass out."

"Marie's not here yet, and she's depending on me."

"Dammit, you don't need this shit. Go home, Maddy. I'll square it with Marie."

DEXTER HAD A decision to make. Loyalty to the dead or concern for the living?

In all of his thirty years on the job, his first consideration had been for the citizens he'd sworn to serve and

justice for the dead, but when he saw Maddy's face, there
was no question.

From the time he'd carried her out of the carnage at her
home when she was six, he had been committed to her
safety and well-being. He'd never forgotten how she had
looked then, her silky blond curls tangled, her big blue
eyes wide with shock, so traumatized that all she could do
was scream when anyone tried to get her out of that house.

But when he'd called her Maddy and reached for her,
she had wrapped her arms around his neck, laid her head
against his cheek, and held on. In the twenty-odd years
since, he couldn't have been more concerned for her wel-
fare if she were his own daughter.

But Maddy on a violent crime scene? Christ-all-Friday,
no matter how much progress she'd made, that was enough
to send her back to the shrink. What the hell was Marie
thinking? She knew Madison's past. If Dexter didn't have
a job to do, he'd personally drive Maddy home, put her to
bed, and stay with her in case of nightmares.

But he did owe the dead, so, arranging for a deputy
to drive her car home, he watched the white Saab disappear up the boulevard. Muttering a curse, he turned to the
crime scene.

THREE

DEXTER'S NEW PARTNER, Detective Felipe Rodrigo, a forty-five-year-old Latino whom Dex had dubbed *Rico*, had questioned the restaurant personnel, and of course, no one had seen anything. Now he was talking to Deputy Hesketh, the first responding officer, and even from several feet away, Dexter could see that the deputy was more than a little irritated.

Shorter than most detectives, Rico had perfected a certain swagger, reminding Dexter of a strutting peacock he'd seen years ago at a theme park. Instead of fanning iridescent feathers, Rico wore tailored suits and spouted procedure to any poor fool he happened to catch unaware. No one liked him. How he'd advanced through the ranks, Dexter couldn't guess. More than once, he'd been tempted to knock the little prig on his ass.

The crime scene techs were taking photos, and the coroner would be arriving soon to declare the cause of death.

Dexter snapped on his latex gloves and crouched down for a closer look at the body.

Male. Caucasian. Late thirties. Blond. Two gunshot wounds to the chest, one to the right temple, all front entrance wounds. Powder burns indicated the perp's close proximity to the victim. Needles, cotton swabs, and the medics' latex gloves still lay where they had left them. Forensics would examine each one for trace evidence. Tattoos covered the victim's knuckles and his black lace-up ankle shoes were prison-issue. The pager under his shirt and the GPS ankle bracelet confirmed it.

Interesting.

Since 2005, when a nine-year-old girl had been raped and murdered in Florida by a convicted sex offender who, it was later revealed, lived across the street, a number of states had passed laws requiring or allowing global tracking. Perhaps it wasn't foolproof, Dexter thought, but it was damned close.

"You see the ankle bracelet?" Rico asked Hesketh.

"High-risk offender," Hesketh said with a slight rolling of eyes.

Dexter held in a sigh. Rico was still playing his game of one-upmanship. As a rookie detective, he had a lot to learn. He just didn't realize it.

"One witness," Hesketh continued, "Brandon Searl, Yucaipa, was having dinner with his wife. When he heard shots, he ran outside, saw the victim down, and administered CPR until paramedics arrived."

His notes were detailed and precise, Dexter observed, and if called to testify, the defense would have a difficult time finding holes in his story.

"You make your notifications?" Dexter asked.

"Yes, sir. The coroner is en route, and I let the mayor and city council know what we have."

Dexter hated all the unofficial protocol, but Yucaipa was a growing community of over fifty thousand in the San Bernardino foothills below Big Bear Lake, and the mayor was active in city affairs. He attended city functions, and it didn't matter if it was a ribbon-cutting ceremony for a new market or a fund-raiser for a school activity. While Yucaipa hadn't suffered from many violent crimes, the newly elected mayor made it known he'd be unhappy if someone asked about a murder and he hadn't been prepped.

Dexter had learned early in his career that it wasn't good to have an unhappy mayor.

The coroner's van pulled into the lot, and a deputy waved him through the yellow tape.

About five-ten, slightly balding, and even in his neatly pressed jumpsuit, San Bernardino County Coroner Julian Goertzen resembled Mikhail Gorbachev and was twice as sharp.

After logging in the time, Dexter joined him and briefed the coroner on what they had so far.

Goertzen opened his evidence collection kit and took photos of the body, the blood splatter on the pavement, the pickup, and the surrounding area. After making a few notes, he knelt, and with Dexter beside him, began his preliminary examination of the body.

"What do you think, Jules?" Dexter asked.

"Two entrance wounds to the left anterior chest may have penetrated the heart. From the size of the wounds, I'd say the perp used a 9mm, possibly hollow-point ammo. Surrounding area is clean, no casings, so I'll have to open him up to be sure."

"A drive-by?"

"The shots were deliberate, Dex, especially the one to the temporal lobe." He pointed to the victim's right temple. "That one was a hard contact discharge, up close and personal. See the gunpowder stippling?"

Rico joined Dexter to observe the pinpoint skin abrasions surrounding the wound. They resembled tiny black pimples.

"Those marks tell me the muzzle was within two feet of the body," Goertzen said for Rico's benefit. "The eccentric margin of abrasion, this area here," he added, pointing to a ring of scraped skin with the abrasion thicker in one area, like a lopsided circle, "tells me the bullet penetrated the skin at an angle. I'd say the assailant discharged two shots at the victim's chest, and then leaned down and fired directly to the temple. Someone wanted him dead."

"Can you estimate the time of death?"

"Rigor's just starting, so I'd say in the last three hours."

Dexter nodded. The timing fit.

"The witness says the perp escaped in the field," Rico told them. All three men gazed at the scrub grass field next to the steakhouse and beyond to the newly paved hillside road and housing tract in various stages of completion.

"Could've gone anywhere," Dexter mused.

"We'll check the area for footprints," Goertzen said, "but it'll take a while."

"Any thoughts about the blood splatter on the pickup?"

"I need time, Dex. You know that."

"Your best guess?"

Goertzen's heavy brows furrowed, and Dexter knew from experience the coroner was already working out the scenario.

"Wrong angle to be from the field. I'd say the shots were fired from the parking lot. Shoes look like Chino's, heels good condition, so I'd guess he got them within the last couple months. Skin's peeling on the knuckles, so the tattoos are recent, perhaps a week. Based on that plus the standard issue shoes, I'd say he's recently released."

Dexter made a note to contact the prison for the exact date.

The victim's pockets yielded a plastic wallet with a California driver's license issued two months earlier to a Jeffrey Hawley, thirty-seven, Calimesa.

After Goertzen wrapped Hawley's head and hands in unlined paper bags and secured them with tape, he nodded at the forensic team. They worked in unison under the floodlights, taking photographs and swabs of the victim's blood, laying tape for a grid search of the parking lot and the dirt field on the west side of the restaurant. They placed tent markers at blood drops and measured the splatter on the pickup to determine the bullets' trajectories.

Dexter wanted to run a search on the victim, so he headed for his Tahoe. A cold breeze blew through the parking lot, ruffling papers and the yellow tape.

Hurrying to catch up, Rico hunched into his suit jacket. "Must've dropped twenty degrees. A suit looks sharp, but it's not as warm as a uniform."

For the first time, Dexter felt a speck of camaraderie for the new detective. "Still spring, Rico, and it gets cold around here in the evenings."

A black SUV pulled into the parking lot and Dexter, recognizing Marie Campbell's 4Runner, paused. She bolted out of the vehicle and rushed over to him, her white-streaked hair bouncing off her shoulders.

"God, what traffic. Where's Madison? I can't reach her on her cell." Marie's sharp eyes took in the scene, darting from the glaring floodlights to the CSI techs. "He died?"

As much as Dexter wanted to let loose with a string of curses, he remembered he was a gentleman. And after working with Marie for over twenty years, hassling the city council for improvements, cosponsoring activities with underprivileged children, he'd never berate her for anything, even if he detested certain aspects of her job.

"I sent her home where she should be," he said after describing her condition. "Here's her camera and notes."

"I need details—"

"You'll get them when I know them," he told her. "As of now, it's the standard fatal shooting in Jimmy's parking lot, assailant unknown, investigation ongoing."

"But—"

"Good night, Marie." He firmly dismissed her and continued to his car. Rico ran to catch up.

"That woman's hanging around, taking photos," he said, checking over his shoulder, his voice incredulous.

"She's a newspaper editor and a professional," Dexter told him, swallowing a snarl, remembering his vow to the captain to get along. "She's done a lot of good for this community and gives her free time whenever someone's in need. She's dedicated and will get this news in the morning's edition even if she has to stay up all night and print it herself. So knock off the attitude."

With Rico in the passenger seat beside him, Dexter ran the ID on his mobile data terminal, and CLETS—the California Law Enforcement Telecommunications System—pulled up a criminal file. Clicking through, Dexter discovered Hawley had a sealed juvenile file and had served nine years for the rape and murder of an eleven-year-old Yucaipa girl before being released from CIM, the California Institution for Men at Chino, a month ago. Presently, he was living with his mother in a mobile home park in Calimesa.

Pedophile. Child murderer.

"So the innocent victim wasn't so innocent after all," Rico said.

Dexter had seen it all before, some victim's boyfriend or father going off half-cocked and taking revenge. While he could understand it, he couldn't condone citizens taking control of the law. That would throw civilization back to the Old West days when people shot each other for a wrong look.

After a quick word to the deputy, he and Rico slid into the backseat of the patrol car. The witness clutched his red cap. The skin around his mouth was white, and Dexter knew the man had reached his limit for tonight. He'd keep the questions brief.

"I know it's been a long night, Mr. Searl," he said after introducing Rico and himself, "but tell me what you saw."

"I already told him everything I know." Searl nodded wearily in the deputy's direction. "Twice."

"You were there?"

"Like I said, the wife and I were inside, having dinner. I heard what I thought was backfire. After all, we're close to the boulevard. Who'd expect gunshots?"

"I understand. How many shots did you hear?"

"Didn't count them, but maybe three, four. That's when I went outside to look. I told my wife to stay inside."

"And? What did you see?"

"At first I didn't see nothing. Then I see this screaming woman bending over something. This guy, he was all shot up."

"You didn't actually witness the shooting?"

"He was down when I got there."

"Did you see anyone running from the scene?"

Searl shook his head. "I didn't see nothing except this guy all shot up, so I pulled the woman down and started CPR. Poor sonofabitch."

"Did you know him?"

"I just saw him inside the restaurant."

"Was the woman with him?"

"I guess. I wasn't paying attention. No reason to, you know?"

"When you pulled her down, did she say anything?"

"She was hysterical, didn't make much sense. You can imagine how she'd be."

"Did she see who shot him?"

"Just that they were talking and someone came running up to them and shot him. Just like that. Then he ran off into the field."

"She said he escaped in the field?"

Searl nodded.

"Who was she?"

"Didn't ask."

"Is she around here now?"

Searl's gaze swept the parking lot. "She's not here, and I haven't seen her since. I was trying to keep the guy alive."

"Can you describe her for me?"

"Can't remember much about her except a big straw hat like ladies wear outside to garden and stuff."

"Was she older or younger than the victim?"

He shrugged. "Older."

"Old enough to be his mother?"

He shrugged again. "I don't know. Older than him. That's all."

After taking Searl's name and number, Dexter released him to go home.

"Let's call it a night, Rico. I'll make the next-of-kin call."

On the way to Calimesa, Dexter thought about the older woman. Was she Hawley's mother? If so, why had she left the scene? Had she panicked at the sound of gunfire and run? Had she felt threatened herself, threatened enough to leave her son behind?

He wanted some answers and he wanted them now, before the trail grew cold.

FOUR

THE FARTHER MADISON got from the crime scene, the stronger she felt. She dropped off the deputy at the station and headed home. Once in her driveway, instead of shutting off the engine, she sat behind the wheel and stared bleakly at her middle unit in the stucco triplex.

Light from the living room lamps glowed through the closed sage drapes, and even though one couldn't tell from the front, a light shone in every room—including the bathroom—and her radio softly played New Age music. By all appearances, someone was home.

Pathetic, Madison knew, absolutely pitiful that a grown woman had to keep her home staged in order to enter it, let alone sleep there. She'd even chosen a middle unit so she wouldn't have to worry about side windows.

Tonight, however, even a fully lit condo didn't give her the sense of security she needed, so she headed for the one place where she felt safe—her grandmother's home, an older two-story frame house nestled in the foothills overlooking the city. It even had a wraparound porch that her grandfather built because Grandma Ella loved to sit with Maddy at night and watch the lights glimmer in the valley. Fairy lights, Gran would tell her, weaving magical stories about fairy godmothers who watched over their charges.

But it was Ella's big, homey kitchen with its yellow walls, butcher-block counters holding glass jars full of cookies, homemade pastas, and spices that Madison loved best. An oak table large enough to seat twelve stood right in the middle of the room, and it was there, during Madison's growing-up years, that she'd help her grandmother roll out dough for noodles, bread, cookies, cakes, and pies. That kitchen was a room full of love and warmth as well as good food, a sanctuary where her grandmother had nurtured her back from the hell in which she'd been thrown at age six.

Madison desperately needed that comfort now.

The hillside home was ablaze with lights and Madison felt a prickling of alarm. Although active in the Women's Club and several charitable organizations, evenings usually found her grandmother tucked on the sofa watching her favorite TV programs.

Then Madison spotted the familiar 1980 Mercedes W126 parked behind Ella's Hyundai. Cora, Ella's best friend for nearly thirty years. No doubt the two women were inside, munching popcorn, "For the fiber, you know," debating the evening's programs. Ella loved a good tearjerker while practical, down-to-earth Cora usually argued for a documentary.

Still, even with Cora visiting, it was unusual for the house to be so bright.

Inside, the Tiffany lamps were lit, the TV dark, and through the archway into the dining room, Madison could see, under the chandelier, the carved dining table set for four with dessert plates, cups, saucers, and even her grandmother's Royal Doulton teapot.

So Gran had been entertaining? Madison felt relief, but why hadn't she known? Since her grandfather's death when she was seventeen, she'd stepped in and helped Ella with most of her activities.

Cora's authoritative voice sounded from the kitchen along with one Madison had never heard. Curious, she walked through and found her grandmother, dressed in a linen pantsuit, taking a can of whipped cream from the fridge. Two pies from the local bakery sat on the oak table.

A woman she didn't know was chatting with Cora and her sister, Clara. Madison was surprised, not only because of the other woman, but because Clara, opposite in every way from her stern sister, preferred evenings at home. Tonight must be special, but again, why hadn't she known?

"This is Adelle Parkins," Ella said, "my best friend from high school. She called this afternoon…late. I was so surprised…" She seemed to prattle, which was unusual for her. Of course one never had much chance to talk when Cora was present.

Madison offered her hand to a woman quite different from her grandmother. Ella loved her salt and pepper hair, telling anyone who asked that she'd never consider coloring it, that she finally had a frost job for free. Adelle wore heavy makeup and her hair was jet black. Or was that a wig?

Ella was soft and round, and about an inch shorter than Madison's five-six. Even sitting, Adelle appeared much taller.

"Your grandmother and I haven't seen each other in years," Adelle explained, "but my son just moved to Riverside and I flew out to see him. I'm so glad I caught Ella at home and not off gallivanting to some exotic place."

"Ella's idea of exotic is the occasional trip to the casino with Sis and me for the seafood buffet," Cora sniffed, sounding even more sharp-tongued than usual.

A bit of jealousy? Madison wondered, sliding onto a wooden chair. Maybe she didn't like the thought of sharing her best friend with a stranger.

"Perhaps next time you visit our area, you can join us." Clara spoke in her usual, barely audible voice.

Life was funny, Madison thought. Gran and Cora,

although so different, got along better than either did with Clara, who was so passive and sweet-looking that she was like a living Kewpie doll. But appearances could be deceiving. Clara was a widow, and although the sisters descended from an orange baron in Old San Bernardino and had never needed to support themselves, Clara spent her adult life teaching English and literature. Cora, on the other hand, was exactly as she appeared. Tall, rail-thin, with metal-frame bifocals, she'd been a secretary at the Marine base, and with her commanding demeanor, she could have been a general.

"Want some pie, honey?" Gran asked, her voice higher pitched than usual. Tighter, as if she were on edge.

"No thanks. I just wanted to see you before I went to bed."

Ella frowned. "What's wrong? You look pale. Did something happen during the review?" She explained to Adelle about Madison's job at the newspaper, her voice filled with pride.

"The three of us often visit the places Madison recommends," Cora said. "Not that we always agree, mind you, but quite often I do." She said it with authority, as if Madison should be flattered. And she was.

"Normally I love it," Madison said with a sigh, "but tonight was something else. Guess you didn't hear that someone was murdered in the parking lot. Marie asked me to cover it until she could get there."

"Murdered?" Both sisters echoed. Everyone looked horrified. "At that Japanese place in Redlands?"

"That's next week. I was at Jimmy's."

Ella dropped the whipped cream. "You were there?"

Madison rose to pick up the can. "I didn't actually see it happen," she said. "When I got there, the paramedics were working on him."

Her grandmother slid into a chair.

"You okay?" Madison filled a glass with water and gave it to her.

Ella struggled to speak, but it was as if all the air in her lungs had been forced out. "What happened?" she finally managed.

"A man was shot." Madison briefly described what happened and about Marie needing her. "I tried to do what she asked, but I didn't get much. I let her down."

"Nonsense," Cora stated. "You're no reporter, and it was preposterous that your editor asked you to stay. At least Detective Quinn had the good sense to send you home."

"Are you okay, Madison?" Clara asked. "You look so pale. Have some tea and pie with us."

"I'm better now, but I'm concerned about Gran."

"It's just been a long evening with her friend unexpectedly showing up." Cora threw a disapproving frown at Adelle. "I'll make sure she gets some rest, so don't worry about that, and I'll drive Adelle to Riverside."

"No!" Ella said, and when everyone looked at her, she blushed. "I'm sorry, Cora. I appreciate the offer, but I might want to spend some time there, meet Adelle's son."

"But, Ella—"

"No, it's okay. I'll be fine by morning."

Cora's sharp features settled into resignation. "Who was murdered?"

Madison didn't want to talk about the evening, especially since it made her grandmother uneasy. But Cora wasn't one to let a subject drop, and, even though Adelle couldn't possibly be interested in local matters, she was paying close attention.

"I don't know who he was, Cora. He didn't look familiar—at least from what I could tell, and Dexter didn't say anything about knowing the guy. But I saw him lying there, and…"

Ella took her granddaughter's hand. "After all you've been through, and now this."

Madison's cell rang, and it was Dexter. "I'm okay," she told him. "I'm at Gran's." They spoke briefly. "He worries about me as if I were still a child," she said after hanging up. "I'm fortunate to have him."

"Why don't you stay over, Maddy? You shouldn't be by yourself tonight."

"Thanks, Gran, but I'll head on home. I have to face Marie in the morning, and all my clothes are at my apartment. I'll pick you up tomorrow afternoon."

"Are you sure you're up to it after what happened tonight?"

"Of course. We don't often get the opportunity to see him."

"If you don't mind me asking," Cora said, "where are you going?"

"To see Senator Stone. He's home from Washington on sick leave. Exhaustion, according to the news, but he still made time for Maddy and me."

"Senator Logan Stone?" Adelle asked, her eyes wide. "You know a United States senator? I'm impressed."

"Don't be, I'm not that important. Years ago when he was the district attorney, he prosecuted that, that—"

"Degenerate," Cora offered.

"Thanks. He worked like a madman to get that degenerate who murdered Madison's parents locked up."

"I heard about that," Adelle said, "and I'm so sorry. It was your daughter, wasn't it?"

"And her husband, but I'd rather not talk about it."

A brown wood spider made its way across the kitchen.

All the ladies, including Madison, silently stared as if it were an invader from another planet.

Cora rose and stomped on it.

"One less undesirable to worry about." She wiped her shoe with a paper towel. "Too bad we can't do the same with Bates."

At Adelle's questioning frown, she explained. "Michael Bates, the man who murdered Ella's daughter and son-in-law. Although he's supposed to serve a life sentence, they just may release him one day. You never know what the courts will do."

"Cora! Drop it," Ella said with the sharpest tone Madison had ever heard. For once, Cora went silent.

Release Bates? Just the thought of him getting out of prison made Madison's heart skip a beat. But she didn't want to worry her grandmother, so she managed to portray a calmness she didn't feel and kissed Ella good night.

Was it possible that her worst nightmare could come true?

FIVE

Deputy Sheriff Hector Gonzales followed Dexter to the senior mobile home park. Most of the yards were brown and overgrown with dandelions, although he noticed an occasional attempt at a flower garden. Even they looked wilted. A dark streetlamp marked a left turn, and only one trailer had outside lights.

"See any numbers?" Dexter radioed, slowly cruising the dim narrow lanes.

"Too dark," the deputy replied, "but I think that's it ahead. That faded pink trailer."

The Hawley place, which, in his headlights, looked at least forty years old, had no flowers, just a brown patch that hadn't been trimmed in years. No gardener there, Dexter thought. But that didn't mean she didn't own a straw hat.

She wasn't truly a suspect, at least not yet. Most mothers didn't kill their offspring—once past the teenage years, he thought wryly. Dexter knew of several times his sister was furious enough at her teenage son to smite him into the next galaxy, but the kid had survived so far. He doubted that a mother, no matter how angry, would accompany her grown son to a restaurant and kill him there. She could've shot him at home. From the looks of the place, he doubted anyone would even notice—or care.

But Mrs. Hawley might know the woman with her son.

He knocked on the torn screen door. The woman who answered appeared to be about sixty, her gray hair a patch of fuzzy corkscrews. She wore pants several sizes too big for her thin frame and a bulky blouse that didn't hide the absence of a bra.

"What now?"

"Detective Dexter Quinn, ma'am." He flashed his shield. "And this is Deputy Sheriff Hector Gonzales. Are you Mrs. Hawley?"

"What's it to you?"

"We'd like to speak to you about your son."

"Jeff's not here, and I don't want to talk to no cops." She backed up and slammed the door shut.

Dexter knocked again. "Please, ma'am, we need to talk."

She cracked open the door. "Look, quit hassling us. Jeff checks in with his parole officer and does everything he's supposed to. I told him he had to or he'd have to leave. He's trying, so why don't you people leave him alone?"

"There's been an incident involving your son."

A long moment passed, and she finally opened the door to a tiny, closed room. Cigarette smoke and the stench of dirty cat litter hung in the air.

"Please sit down, Mrs. Hawley." Dexter spoke quietly. "I'm sorry to tell you—"

"He's dead, isn't he?" At Dexter's nod, her hostility crumbled. Her eyes filled and overflowed.

Dexter dismissed her as a possible suspect. Unless his instincts from years on the job were dead wrong, he'd swear she knew nothing about the murder. But if she hadn't been the woman with the straw hat, who had it been?

It never got easier, so Dexter and Gonzales waited awkwardly while she wept.

"How did he die?" It was little more than a whisper.

"He was shot—" Dexter began.

"It was that poor little girl's father, wasn't it? Jeff was my son, but he was…cruel. What he did to that girl's body just wasn't decent." She shook her head as if it was all beyond her. "I tried to raise him right, but somewhere, he went wrong."

According to the notes Dexter had taken about Jeff Hawley's conviction, he had tortured and murdered Angela Jordan, an eleven-year-old local girl. And he'd only spent nine years in the Chino Institution for Men. Nine years. Dexter wasn't sure he wouldn't want to kill him too.

"Did Mr. Jordan threaten your son?" he asked Hawley's mother now.

"Said he'd kill him."

"When was that?"

"When Jeff's lawyer did that thing to get him a lighter sentence."

"Plea bargain?"

She shrugged.

"There was a woman, an older woman according to witnesses, with your son when he left the restaurant. Do you have any idea who it could be?"

"A woman? Jeffrey didn't have any friends. Someone got his story wrong."

"Did he attend any social functions where he could've met someone?"

"He didn't go nowhere," she told him. "About drove me nuts. I couldn't get him out of the house except to go to that steakhouse. He loved it there, went most every night. Said for once, he could eat all he wanted."

"Did he talk about meeting a woman there?"

"He didn't talk to me, wouldn't even look at me most of the time. Ever since he was released last month, we don't talk. It was like he blamed me for everything. What did I do? Maybe I smacked him too much, but I tried to raise him right. It's not easy being all alone."

"Is there someone who can identify your son for you?"

"No one." She sounded so dejected that Dexter wished he could help. Everyone should have at least one person to love—and who loved them. He wondered if he'd wind up like her, unloved and alone.

"If you'll get your things," he said gently, "Deputy Gonzales will take you to your son."

Dexter drove out of the court and took a deep breath of the cool, evening air.

His next stop was the Spencer Jordan residence in Yucaipa. Dexter gave a moment's thought to calling Rico, but he was too tired to tolerate the dickhead. He might have to suffer some hand-slapping for not doing so, but he'd face it in the morning.

AFTER CALLING TO make sure her grandmother was okay, Madison turned off the radio, and, leaving most of the lights on, slid into bed.

She tried to sleep, but the night sounds seemed louder than normal. A nest of birds chirped in the lemon tree outside her back window. Great. If she didn't get some sleep, she'd be a zombie at work tomorrow. Her head pounded. She felt like throwing a can at the tree. Who ever heard of birds singing at night?

Suddenly, all noises stopped. Even the fridge went silent. Listening intently, Madison sat up. A creak sounding just like someone walking in the living room made her mouth go dry.

Someone was in the house!

She almost bolted for the closet as she'd done all those years ago, peeking through the louvered doors, trying not to make a sound as he'd searched for her, throwing back the covers, stooping to peer under her bed.

He straightened and looked around the room.

His eyes caught hers.

He smiled, a creepy, skin-shivering smile.

"Gotcha," he whispered, moving toward her.

She wet the floor.

Distant sirens wailed, growing louder as they moved closer.

He stopped to listen.

"I'll be back." He flashed that sly smile and disappeared through the door.

Panic pushed the memory aside. If he were here and had broken in, she needed to think, to stay alive. Pulling open the nightstand drawer, she took out the handgun Dexter's former partner had helped her to buy. Holding the .38 revolver in front of her, she waited, then after hearing nothing more, she crept through the hallway and into the living room.

Nothing had been moved. Magazines were still neatly stacked on the coffee table, wing chairs angled just so, the lamps exactly in the middle of end tables. The front door was closed and locked, dead bolts in place.

Just to make sure no one was there, she made her way through the condo, still holding her weapon, checking every corner, throwing open every closet door, flipping on every light. She checked the sliding glass doors leading from the kitchen to the courtyard in back and found them closed and locked, the steel rod still in the track. In order to get in, an intruder would've broken through, and she would have heard the crash.

Feeling a little foolish, she poured a glass of water from the polished fridge door and began to think rationally. Even if someone had broken in, it couldn't have been Bates. He was still in prison, locked up so he couldn't hurt anyone else. The talk about his release was just that. Wasn't it?

Back in bed, she couldn't keep her eyes closed.

The night noises came alive again, and she lay awake and guarded against the night.

SUPERIOR COURT JUDGE Joseph Lewon didn't sound happy when Dexter called at two in the morning, but it was part of the job.

Dexter asked for and was issued a search warrant that included the house, vehicles, and the surrounding property such as detached garages, workshops, and the lawn itself. Too many defense attorneys shot down evidence obtained in a location that hadn't been listed on the document.

Warrant in hand, Dexter, accompanied by three deputies, knocked on the Jordan residence door, trying not to wake the neighbors in the upscale Chapman Heights home facing the golf course. When no one responded, he knocked louder. Inside, a large dog barked, then an upstairs light flipped on. The man who opened the door was in his early forties, his robe slung over pajama bottoms, dark hair sticking straight up in back like an errant cowlick. He glared at Dexter.

"Who the hell are you? Do you realize it's almost three in the morning?"

"Are you Spencer Jordan?" Dexter flashed his shield and identified himself.

"Homicide! What could you possibly want here?"

"I have a search warrant issued in the investigation of a homicide that occurred earlier this evening, and I'd like your cooperation. May we come in?"

"Search warrant? For me?"

"Afraid so."

"Homicide? Who was killed?"

"Jeffrey Hawley."

Jordan appeared stunned. His mouth actually dropped

open. "Jeff Hawley," he repeated cautiously, "the scum who murdered my daughter? He's dead? Really dead?"

At Dexter's nod, Jordan broke out in a smile and threw open the door.

"Come in! I'll even open all the drawers and cabinets for you." He flipped on the living room lights and yelled upstairs. "Gerri! Come on down! Got wonderful news!"

Dexter had seen a myriad of reactions to a search warrant, but this one was a doozer. He wouldn't be surprised if Jordan did handsprings across the room.

He dismissed Jordan as a suspect. He'd follow through with the necessary questioning and weapon's search, but instinct told Dexter that Jordan was innocent.

However, when Mrs. Jordan glided down the stairs, her pale blond hair only slightly disheveled, her floor-length blue robe shining like silk, he wondered if she were involved. Wives didn't always tell their husbands everything.

Seated in the living room large enough to hold his entire studio apartment, Dexter questioned the couple while the deputies searched the house.

"Mrs. Jordan, do you own one of those large straw hats that ladies wear outside?"

"I don't go outside in the daylight, Detective Quinn. I'm one of those unfortunates who are allergic to the sun." Dexter noticed her smooth skin. Not only was it flawless, but it was so light it was almost albino.

"May I ask your whereabouts around six this evening?"

"Detective—" Mr. Jordan began.

"It's okay, Spence." She patted his hand. "My husband and I were at a dinner party raising funds for a local benefit, Detective. If that's when that monster was killed, I have about three hundred witnesses who can testify I was there." Her eyes filled, but she kept her gaze on Dexter. "I've often thought about killing him over the years, even fantasized about stabbing him in the heart and watching him die, but my belief system says murder is a sin. I may rejoice that he's dead and no longer a threat to anyone else, but I didn't kill him."

Dexter believed her.

But who killed Hawley? And why hadn't the woman with him come forward?

SIX

Madison braced herself before entering the office the next morning. Instead of looking forward to finding an obscure new restaurant to review, she dreaded facing Marie.

Even though her editor had been a fantastic mentor, patient and encouraging when instructing, overlooking foibles she didn't tolerate with her reporters, this morning Madison dragged her steps. Leaving a crime scene without all the information was a major sin at a newspaper, and a throbbing headache and scratchy eyes after only three hours sleep didn't help.

As usual, the office was noisy with ringing phones, clacking computer keys, conversations among the four reporters and the two ads-salespeople, and the accountants, as usual, nagging reporters for time sheets and expenses.

All work stopped when Madison entered, and everyone looked at her.

"What?" She looked down at her trousers. "Did I forget my skirt? Oh, wait, I don't wear skirts. So what is it?"

Several coworkers grinned. "Good job," Madison heard. "Atta girl."

"Madison Young, star reporter."

Making her way to her desk as quickly as her pounding head would allow, Madison flushed. "Oh, for heaven's sake, everyone go back to work."

"Oooh, touchy this morning, are we?" Sue, a red-haired accountant, said with a grin.

Madison made a face and Sue laughed. She dug in her

drawer for aspirin; neatly filed below were copies of the year's previous reviews, new restaurants to check, and ones outside the area that looked interesting.

"Guess you had an exciting night." Steve, the senior reporter, slung one arm over the back of his desk chair and leaned back, ready to hear all the gory details.

Madison groaned. Divorced and single, Steve was the typical Latin ladies' man in his prime—at least according to him. He was also devoted to his job. Too bad he wasn't as devoted to child-support. Madison had heard him on the phone many times, making excuses why he hadn't sent a payment. This morning she was in no mood to spar with him.

Marie sat at her computer behind the inner office door, her corner desk messy as usual with scattered notes and a paper plate full of crumbles from her morning muffins. Pinned to the walls were drawings the local schoolchildren had made during outings she'd sponsored and attended as a counselor, as well as plaques and scrolls from various organizations thanking her for her unending participation and service.

Madison slid to the chair beside her.

"I'm so sorry," she began.

"You did good, kid. Just look at this." Marie pushed the morning's paper at her, and Madison caught a glimpse of the fire truck and ambulance from last night.

"I don't want to see it."

"You're a natural, girl. Wish you'd reconsider training as a cub."

"No way. Not only do I want to stay as far away from that stuff as I can, but there are too many variables in that sort of reporting. At least at a review, I can control what happens."

"You change your mind, you let me know. And by

the way, don't waste any sympathy on that guy. He was a pedophile just out of prison. Not only did he rape an eleven-year-old child, but he tortured her and dumped her body in the ravine off Highway 38 to Big Bear. She was found not far from your grandmother's property. I'd say he deserved what he got."

An hour later, just as Madison finished her research on a new seafood restaurant in Moreno Valley, her cell phone rang. The ID said it was Greg Wright, the man she'd dated a few times.

Should she answer it? He wanted to *step up their relationship*, and Madison wanted it to stay right where it was. After her short marriage ended in divorce three years earlier—her fault, she knew, because of her paranoia—she hadn't dated until Greg. Now she wasn't sure she wanted to see anyone. She had enough trouble living with herself.

After a few more rings and a questioning glance from Steve, she took the call.

"Madison, I just read what happened at Jimmy's last night. Are you all right?"

"Other than a sleepless night, I'm fine."

"How about I pick you up after work and we'll have a nice, relaxing dinner? I'll even let you pay."

He was teasing her, although it was true that she often insisted on going Dutch, just to make sure he remembered they were just friends.

"Thanks, Greg, but I've made plans with my grandmother this afternoon, then I'll probably grab some takeout and eat in front of the TV. I'm exhausted."

"Tell you what. Come on up and I'll prepare dinner, even make eggplant parmesan, and you can nap. I'll wake you when it's ready, and I'll even do the dishes. How's that for an offer you can't refuse?"

Madison wavered. It did sound tempting.

They'd met six months before when he'd opened a family-style restaurant in Oak Glen—a fourteen-acre apple-growing community in the foothills of the San Bernardino Mountains about six miles east of Yucaipa—and she wrote a glowing review. Since then, they'd seen each other occasionally, and while she'd enjoyed the outings and wasn't seeing anyone else, she wasn't ready for anything serious.

And she'd never invited Greg into her home, wouldn't allow anyone in except Dex and her grandmother.

"Thanks, Greg. I appreciate the offer, but maybe another time."

After she hung up, she felt disgusted with herself. She had just turned down a wonderful evening with a young man who seemed interested in her, all because she found it difficult to form an emotional bond with anyone other than Gran and Dexter. Her therapist had tried to help her reach out to people, to trust again, but she still hesitated. And now, instead of sharing a wonderful dinner with Greg, she'd stay home behind her locked doors and windows.

Safe, yes. But living? Madison didn't think so.

On his way to the station at ten that morning, Dexter picked up two cups of coffee from a drive-thru and loaded them with several packets of sugar and several containers of cream. After only an hour's sleep, he needed something rich in his blood to get it moving.

The scorching sun didn't help his scratchy eyes. The mercury had already hit ninety and was expected to top off near a hundred.

At the garage, he checked for Rico's sedan, hoping he'd come and gone. His body screamed with exhaustion and every muscle ached, and he simply didn't have enough energy to pacify hurt feelings.

In the squad room, dubbed the bull pen after the place

where relievers on a pro baseball team waited to go into the game, Detective Bob Tieche, an old-timer who'd mentored Dexter, sat with a phone to his ear, nibbling on a Danish. Tieche's partner of a year, Christine Swensen, a tall, slim, blonde, was a perfect contrast to pudgy, bald Tieche. The pair, dubbed Tish and Chris, looked comical together, but they were a top-notch team. True to his Taurus sign, Tish stubbornly hung on to an investigation, probing leads, checking tiny details from every possible angle, and when one played out, pursuing another.

Tish and Chris looked up and grinned.

"What?" Dexter asked. "Did I forget to zip my fly?"

Chris grinned and went back to her files. Tish rolled his eyes toward Rico, who, as usual, was at his desk. Even sitting, Rico looked rigid, his back straight as if he didn't want to wrinkle his finely tailored suit.

He glanced up when Dexter entered the room and scowled, his eyes so dark they were almost black. Points of red highlighted his olive skin, and his lips were slashed in anger. But instead of threatening, he looked as if something had his balls in a vice.

Ah, Christ, Dexter thought. Rico's got a hair up his ass. Guess he'd have to deal with it later, but not now when all he wanted to do was give his report to the captain, check Hawley's background for possible leads, and knock off early and get some rest. He was getting too old for all this shit. At least the captain would be reasonable.

Captain Jessie Silva was pouring steaming cocoa from a thermos when Dexter entered, and the room smelled like rich chocolate.

"Want some?" he asked, his voice as smooth as his Native American features.

"Got my coffee, thanks." Dexter dropped onto the chair.

"Good chocolate, fresh milk, sugar, some water. Next

to pure water, it's the best thing you can drink. You might try it sometime. It'll do you good instead of that sludge you torture your guts with." Silva took a couple of small sips from his mug and sat back to listen while Dexter filled him in on last night's events.

"What now?" Silva asked when Dexter finished his report.

"I could knock on a few doors. Might try Hawley's parole officer, see if he has any insight."

Silva nodded, and Dexter was about to make his escape when the captain spoke in the deceptively calm voice that all the detectives dreaded.

"Detective Quinn," Silva said, bringing Dexter to a halt. "Do you have any idea what I've had to listen to this morning because of you? What tirade the entire station had to hear?"

Even irritated, Silva's voice was conversational. Like his Cahuilla ancestors, he made calm decisions after weighing all possibilities. Over the years Dexter had cooled his heels a number of times while waiting for the captain's okay in one matter or another, but the captain had earned his respect, an honor Dexter awarded to few men.

He knew Silva expected a response, although experience told him to run like hell. "What?"

"Rico," Silva said. "I'm sure, if you think about it, you can guess how it went."

"Captain—"

"I don't like tirades," Silva told him. "It upsets the balance of nature. Balance, Dexter. If someone cuts you off on the freeway, you get irritated, but now you add a certain amount of frustration because you can't pull the asshole out of the vehicle and beat the shit out of him. So what do you do to maintain balance? You cut someone else off. They, in turn, cut another poor soul off, and the cycle continues."

"Cap—"

"As it is on the freeway, so it is here in the bull pen. I have to listen to a tirade from your new partner, I get irritated at you. When I get irritated at one of my detectives, although I try not to stoop to such levels, I sometimes seek revenge. I cancel vacations."

Dexter came to full alert.

"Aren't you scheduled for a vacation in the near future, Detective Quinn?"

"You wouldn't."

Silva leisurely sipped his cocoa. "Thirteen days from now, isn't it?"

Thirteen days until Dexter's vacation, and for the first time in years, he had plans. He was going back to his hometown, a small coal-mining town in southwestern West Virginia.

He'd only visited once since joining the Navy after high school. His parents had moved to California when the underground mines played out, and his grandfather had died years ago of black lung disease. Most of the buildings in the once-vibrant town were boarded up, and the two movie theaters were long gone. The hollow where he'd been born was inaccessible, gated at the mouth by another coal-mining company that had torn down the houses and taken over operations in the area. About the only things left were a few homes scattered along the highway leading into the ghost town.

But far beyond the decay was the tragedy of the mountaintop removal. His beloved Appalachian Mountains were being decimated in several states, the tops blown off because it was the fastest, cheapest way to extract coal, the rubble filling once-pristine streams. From the air, the barren area looked like a Martian landscape, and he hadn't been back.

But memories of his childhood had been pulling at him and he longed to walk the forests and rivers once more. Might be old age, a yearning for what had passed away, but he had to go, at least one last time. Maybe it was his growing need to connect to something, anything.

His marriage had only lasted four years, and his one serious relationship after that had dissolved after a few missed dinners, with him coming home, exhausted, at five in the morning. Most people thought doctors had strange hours; they had no clue about a homicide detective's life.

"Okay, Captain," he said wearily. "What's the problem with Rico?"

"He's unhappy that you left him out of the process last night."

Dexter opened his mouth to speak, but once again, Silva didn't give him the opportunity.

"I don't want to hear reasons or excuses. Just realize, like it or not, he's your new partner. I want him to learn from the best and that's you. Now get the hell out of here and fix the problem, Dexter. I don't want to be unhappy."

GOLDEN LIGHT FROM wall sconces glowed on rich cherrywood paneling. Matching floor lamps illuminated the corners of the book-lined room. The soft chatter of light conversation came from seven men and women who sat around a highly polished table enjoying a buffet breakfast. All were dressed in tailored suits—except for an eighty-year-old man whose alias in the Ruby Red Society was Number Three. He wore jeans and a bottle-green smoking jacket with shawl lapels. Although he hadn't smoked his pipe in fifteen years, he told everyone he kept his favorite cherry-scented tobacco in his pocket—just in case.

A ruby-red glass basket sat on the table within arm's

reach of the chairperson sitting at the head of the table. In front of each member lay a stack of four manila files.

A gray-haired man in a crisp white shirt and black trousers served coffee and cleared the dishes when the members were finished. Once he left the room, the chairperson—known as Jericho One or simply Jericho—picked up the top file. All conversation ceased.

"I'm pleased to announce the elimination of Jeffrey Hawley, case number four-eight-fifty-six, has been successfully completed."

Murmurs of congratulations wove around the table and Jericho smiled. "While we would have preferred a little less risk, we all know that due to circumstances, our plan for this particular target was the best possible course. Are there any comments?"

When no one spoke, the chairperson made a notation on the first file, placed it on the table, and picked up the next one.

"If you'll open the next file, you'll find the next case for consideration is that of William 'Willy Boy' Martin, age twenty-seven, Yuma, Arizona. Resided with his wife, Sharon, twenty-two, and infant daughter, Jennifer.

"On January thirteenth of this year, Martin was arrested for the murder of his wife and daughter. He told police his daughter had cried all day and he couldn't hear the TV, so he picked her up by her ankles and shook her as one would shake a towel. He then threw the body into the corner of the room. Mrs. Martin screamed and ran to the baby. The noise was too much for Martin, he told police, so he got his gun and shot her five times. Neighbors reported gunshots, and Mrs. Martin was pronounced dead at the scene. Mr. Martin was apprehended several blocks away."

"Well, I'm certainly glad to hear that," Number Six said. "But I have a feeling that's not the end of the story."

"You're right," Jericho told him. "Martin has a history of violence. At the age of eight, he was in counseling for setting a live dog on fire, 'just to see what it would do while burning,' and he spent four years in custody until the age of eighteen for the murder of his friend, James Roche. According to the records, the boys had been taking turns batting a softball. When James refused to give up the bat, Martin forcibly took it from him and beat James over the head with it until he was dead.

"The justice system has been very good to Mr. Martin." Jericho poured a cup of steaming coffee. "He served only four years as a juvenile for the murder of the young boy, and as an adult, was indicted on two counts of first-degree murder for the death of his wife and daughter. However, he later recanted his confession, and his defense attorney charged and proved to the court's satisfaction that forensics had mishandled the evidence. The charges were dropped and Mr. Martin was released from custody. He's now seeing a woman with a three-year-old daughter.

"Ladies and gentlemen, I'll pass the ruby bowl for your vote."

"You know what mine will be," Number Three said, taking his pipe from his jacket and inserting it, unlit, between his teeth.

"Yes, Three," Jericho replied with a smile. "None of us have any doubt."

"Damned right. I believe in the old saying, 'Turnabout is fair play.' In my opinion, Mr. Martin should have the opportunity to see what it feels like to burn to death."

Number Five spoke up. "You must remember we're not a malicious society. We're for justice, not revenge."

"Once a spoilsport, always a spoilsport," Number Three replied with good-natured grumbling. "You won't let me have any fun. But you're right. I suppose we must stick to our Code."

Jericho passed the ruby bowl to the member seated on the immediate right, and it made its way around the table to collect the votes.

Jericho tabulated the results and announced the planned extermination of the man who, in the opinion of everyone around the table, deserved to die.

"Thank you for your votes. We'll take a short break before we proceed to the next file."

SEVEN

MADISON ESCORTED HER grandmother down the hillside stairs.

"Where's your friend?" she asked, helping the older woman into the Saab.

"I drove, uh, Adelle back to…to Riverside this morning."

She seemed unusually flustered, and Madison was concerned about her grandmother's sudden decline in health. Until the last couple of months, Ella had worked crossword puzzles in ink. Madison made a mental note to suggest a checkup.

She took the scenic route to Redlands over Sand Canyon Road that Ella liked, enjoying the green hills that would soon turn brown in the scorching summer sun. They passed the few remaining orange groves.

"How did it go this morning?" Ella asked. "Did you get some rest last night?"

"Marie told me the victim was a child murderer and pedophile, so I don't feel quite so sorry for him. But still, people shouldn't go around taking the law into their own hands."

"There are some I'd like to shoot," Ella said quietly, staring out the side window.

Madison glanced at her grandmother's strained face. She couldn't recall much about her parents' murder and the trial, only that it nearly put Ella into the hospital and left Madison with memory fragments and terrifying dreams.

After a lifetime of therapy, she could still hear the sound of her mother's screams as clearly as she had that night.

But no amount of therapy had helped her remember her mother—a fugue state or selective amnesia due, her shrink believed, to not only the trauma, but also to Madison's feelings of guilt.

Michael Bates had been apprehended outside of the Youngs' home, bloody knife on his person, jewelry and cash from the home in a knapsack. He was serving life at San Quentin, and each time he'd been eligible for parole, Dexter, accompanied by Senator Stone when he could take the time, testified to the cruelty in which Madison's parents had been slaughtered.

Madison had never visited their graves.

Concerned about her grandmother, Madison said nothing more. She owed Ella so much and wanted nothing more than to care for her, to take her on the trips she'd sacrificed to raise Madison. She'd even suggested moving back in after her failed marriage, but Ella wouldn't hear of it.

"You have your own life, Maddy. Get out and live it."

Madison owned her own home, worked at a job she loved, and had begun dating again—if you could call three dates in two years dating. But she wasn't sure she was living.

Now, crossing Redlands Boulevard, Madison drove down a palm-and-oak-lined street housing older bungalows and Victorians, each home looking as if it had been freshly painted.

"How's your young man?" Ella asked. "Any good news yet?"

"Please. I don't have a young man and I don't want one."

"That young man you've been seeing. What's his name again?"

"Greg and I have only gone to dinner a few times,"

Madison said, not bothering to hide her exasperation. "Don't make it into something it's not. Okay?"

"Did I tell you he stopped by one afternoon to introduce himself? I thought that was a fine thing to do."

Madison jerked the wheel and almost drove onto the sidewalk.

"He did what?"

"Shall I drive, dear?" Ella asked innocently.

"Don't change the subject. When did Greg stop by? And what did you two discuss, as if I didn't know."

"We had cookies. Peanut butter is his favorite, you know. I'll give you the recipe."

"Oh, my, God. You two are cooking up something besides cookies. Gran, I love you, but stay out of my nonexistent love life. Please."

"He's a good man, Maddy. I could tell that right away."

"Gran—"

"You're young and beautiful, and you need to get out of that house and explore what life has to offer. Go out with Greg. Let him be part of your life."

"I'm not going to talk about it any longer, and if you insist, you can get out and walk."

Her grandmother laughed. "If there's one thing I know, Maddy, dear, is that you'd never abandon me, and that's part of the problem. Quit worrying about me and concentrate on your own life. Get married and give me some great-grandchildren."

"No one could stand living with me." Madison's tone changed. Her voice was barely audible. "Ted walked out in less than a year, said I was too controlling, too much of a shrew if I couldn't run things the way I wanted. And he was right. The biggest fight we had was when he forgot to lock the bedroom window."

"Well, there is that. Have you considered going back into therapy?"

"Dr. King didn't cure me in all the years I went, so I'm not about to waste more time and money on a hopeless cause."

"I'm not sure I agree, Maddy. Even if it's—"

"Gran, I love you, but I don't want to talk about it. I just want to have a nice visit with the senator without a grilling about my personal life. Just a nice relaxing chat and something good to nibble on. Besides, I don't know if I could change even if I wanted to."

The senator's red-tiled rooftop was barely visible through the trees lining the iron fence set in concrete. At the security gate, Madison punched in the new code that had been telephoned to her grandmother the day before, and they wound through grounds shaded by maples, oaks, and sycamore trees.

A circular driveway led to the front of the L-shaped home, and outside the office wing, young cherry trees were in bloom. In the back, Madison knew, a swimming pool sparkled in front of tree-shaded guest quarters.

Mr. Chauncey opened the door.

"Nice to see you again," he said with a smile. Dressed in his usual navy-blue trousers, crisp white shirt, and blue vest, he'd served as a butler as long as Madison could remember.

"Are you sure he's up to a visit?" she asked. "I understand he's not well, and Gran and I wouldn't want to intrude."

"Oh, no, Miss Young," he assured her, leading them through the massive living room to the cozy anteroom outside the senator's office. "The senator mentioned he was looking forward to seeing you both. He'll be with you shortly." He withdrew from the room.

When Ella settled into her favorite chair, a Queen Anne with a footstool, Madison took the upholstered sofa, and, as she'd always done, turned to look at the framed photo standing on the end table. The tender moment when a much-younger senator was holding his infant son and leaning toward his wife always intrigued her, no matter how many times she had seen it. The couple looked at each other with such love that she'd envied them. Even today, many years after an accident had tragically torn his family from him, the senator's eyes still reflected the pain of that loss whenever he spoke of them.

Would she ever experience such love?

"I hope I didn't keep you waiting." Senator Logan Stone walked into the room from his open office door, his long legs taking slower steps than normal. Instead of his usual suit, he wore pleated khakis and a polo shirt, the dark indigo shade setting off his perfectly groomed silver hair.

Madison thought he looked fantastic, especially for a man in his sixties whose doctor sent him home for some much-needed rest. He seldom wore short sleeves, she knew, preferring to cover the jagged six-inch scar on his right arm. He never discussed it, but his act of bravery in combat was well-known.

During visits when she was a child, she'd long to climb onto his lap and loosen his collar as she'd once done for her father. And she had suffered through an adolescent crush when she was thirteen. Now she thought of him as a family friend, not as dear as Dexter, but as someone she trusted and admired.

After giving each woman a brief, informal hug, the senator settled into a large wing chair opposite the sofa.

"I'm so glad we had this opportunity to get together," he told them. "Ready for some tea?"

As was the custom, the housekeeper pushed a scrolled

tea cart into the room, and Madison didn't realize how hungry she was until she saw the food.

The top tier held a teapot, cups and saucers, a tray with several blends of teas, silverware, and all the sides, including sliced lemon. A variety of finger sandwiches and scones occupied the second tier, and on the third, cookies, tarts, cakes, and other goodies sat alongside Madison's can of soda and a bowl of ice.

He never forgot.

The senator served the tea and Madison helped herself to her favorite, a cranberry scone with a heaping spoon of freshly made Devonshire cream.

"Just as wonderful as always, Senator. I don't know what I'd do if your cook ever retired."

"She'll never leave, Madison. I've bribed her into the next century. So tell me, how are you both?"

"Madison witnessed a murder last night," Ella told him. "At Jimmy's Steakhouse."

For a moment, the silence in the room was electrifying.

AFTER COMPLETING THE morning's paperwork, Dexter suggested grabbing a bite to eat. Rico had made a point of ignoring him, and while Dexter couldn't bring himself to apologize, a late lunch was the next thing. Even that didn't settle well, but he knew the captain meant every word of his threat if he didn't make nice to the asshole.

"I still have paperwork to complete," a sullen Rico said, "although obviously not as much as *you* do."

Tish and Chris snickered, but at Dexter's glare, they bent their heads to their own paperwork.

"Come on, Rico," Dexter said. "Give me a break. I spent a long time without a partner, and it'll take some getting used to."

Rico kept writing.

Damn. Dexter glanced up to see Silva, cup in hand, watching the drama through the inner-office window. Dexter shrugged helplessly, which was quite a feat. He'd never been helpless in his life and Silva knew it.

"Come on, buddy." He about choked on that one. "Let's grab a bite and then check with Hawley's parole officer."

"Well…if you make sure it doesn't happen again."

That did it. Vacation or no vacation, he wasn't going to grovel. He grabbed his jacket from the back of the chair and stormed out of the room.

"Where do you want to eat?" Rico asked, running after him.

An hour later at the state offices in San Bernardino, Dexter and Rico waited a few moments for Hawley's parole officer to finish an interview.

Mike Taggert's cubicle was one of several in the large room, and over the noise of conversations and phones ringing, Dexter and Rico introduced themselves and took seats.

His white shirt wrinkled and sleeves rolled to his elbows, Taggert presented the perfect picture of a harried government employee. He grabbed a red file with Hawley's name scribbled on the front.

"Sorry, detectives, I can't help you. I've only been assigned to Hawley a few weeks. And with this kind of backlog," he swept his hand over the stacks of files, "I've only talked to him once."

"Any clues to his social activities?" Dexter asked.

"GPS report showed no unusual actions, no attempts to approach restricted zones. Since he was high-risk, we tracked him with real-time monitoring for the first month, then downgraded him to a daily basis. Got the impression he was a loner. No friends, no activities."

"He had someone," Dexter said, and filled him in on

the woman with the straw hat, careful to let Rico contribute to the conversation.

"Guess he was trying to readjust to civilian life," Taggert said.

"Someone made sure he didn't adjust to anything."

Back in the Tahoe, Dexter received a call from Josh Gidding on his cell phone and stepped out of the car. As a member of the Adult Parole Operations with California's Department of Corrections and Rehabilitation, Josh never called to pass the time of day.

"Bates' hearing got pushed up to tomorrow," he told Dexter. "This time it looks good."

Damn.

"Have to make a quick trip north," Dexter told Rico, fastening his seat belt. "You do what you can on the Hawley case, and I'll be back tomorrow evening or the next day."

"What's up?"

"A ghost from the past."

"I DIDN'T ACTUALLY witness the murder, Gran. I arrived afterward. Besides, Senator Stone doesn't want to hear about the shooting," If Madison had ever been exasperated with her grandmother, it was now. She felt better once she had eaten, but her temples still throbbed.

"I most certainly do, Madison. Anything that concerns your family is of interest to me. I'd heard about the incident, of course, but had no idea you were involved. Please tell me all about it."

There was no way Madison could refuse a request from such a longtime friend. When she finished telling him about last night, he seemed horrified.

"Good God, Madison. Your grandmother is right— you should not have been involved. I'm surprised at your editor."

Madison closed her eyes. "Once again, my editor had no other choice. It was a big story and if no one had been there at all, the paper would have been horribly embarrassed. After everything Marie has done for me, I wanted to help. So please, as a favor to me, let's just drop the subject."

"As you wish, my dear. Your grandmother and I have some catching up to do. As you know, my last bit of legislation is stalled again. Would you care to join us in the office?"

Normally, Madison loved to assist the senator, felt honored to contribute to drafting the senator's legislation. His previous one, HQEV5454, allowing the prosecution to submit the defendant's complete criminal record at trial, had died in committee, but he kept working, and she and Ella had been strong supporters, working with the senator when he was in town, keeping in touch with his staff by phone or mail when he was in Washington.

But not today. Even with the spectacular view of the cherry trees outside of the senator's office, Madison couldn't face spending the afternoon inside.

"If you don't mind, I'd rather stroll the grounds. It's beautiful outside, and I'll enjoy the fresh air." She didn't mention that she needed to be alone. Something was nagging at her and she had to try to figure out what was wrong. Ever since Ella mentioned the shooting at Jimmy's, she'd felt a tension in the air, a feeling unusual in the senator's home.

AFTER GETTING THE official okay from Captain Silva to attend the parole hearing at San Quentin, Dexter caught the next flight out of Ontario for Oakland. Even though it only took a couple of hours, he left early to make sure nothing came up to prevent him from attending.

He and the senator had testified to Bates' brutality at

the hearing a year ago, and Dexter was surprised that another was scheduled so soon. But with the state's budget crisis and prison overcrowding, hearings were pushed up and prisoners released without serving their full terms.

He'd called Senator Stone to inform him of the hearing, but the senator felt too weak to make the trip.

Dexter watched the shifting cloud formations and thought back twenty years to the crime that still gave Madison nightmares.

She hadn't witnessed her parents' murder or been physically injured, thank God, but she was left with emotional scars that time and therapy hadn't lessened.

Instead of running to her mother when awakened by her screams, Madison had been so terrified by the sound that she hid in the closet. Not only did she have to cope with losing her parents, but she carried the burden that she hadn't tried to help, as if a six-year-old could've done anything except get herself killed. While her therapist had helped her to work through the logistics, she had never recovered from the guilt of that night. Or the fear.

And Dexter understood. Mrs. Young's screams must have been unbearable. He'd seen crime scenes before, but nothing that heinous, not in his county, not in his town.

Talk about nightmares.

Small burn marks on Mrs. Young's eyelids, face, and breasts indicated torture with a cigarette, then she'd been sexually assaulted and stabbed multiple times, the wounds so deep in her stomach that she'd almost been disemboweled.

Mr. Young had been bound and gagged on the floor next to the bed, his head propped against the wall, his legs drawn up. The medical examiner speculated that he died about a half hour after his wife and might have been forced to watch his wife's torture and murder. He'd bled out after his carotid artery had been severed, his throat slashed so savagely that only a few tendons kept his head attached.

The neighbor on the south side of the house had heard the screams and called the police. Dexter had been one of the responding officers, and during a search of the house, found Maddy in her closet, terrified, reeking of urine, unable to move. If there was anything to be thankful for, it was that she hadn't seen her parents' bodies.

When Bates had been apprehended, records proved he'd been arraigned on a burglary and murder charge two months before, but the case had been thrown out of court because of an illegal search of his premises.

But the pattern was there.

God help the citizens of California if that monster were allowed back on the streets.

"GRAN, IS THERE anything I can do for you?" Madison asked, back inside Ella's hillside home. "You look so pale, and you haven't said a word since leaving the senator's house. Would you like something to drink?"

Ella leaned her head against the back of the sofa and closed her eyes. "I'm fine, Maddy. Why don't you run along, now. I'm sure you have things to do."

"What's wrong, Gran? This isn't like you. Are you angry that I didn't help with the senator's bill?"

"No, dear. Of course not. I'd never be angry with you. It's just, uh, between Adelle showing up unexpectedly and visiting the senator today, I'm exhausted. And this sudden heat doesn't help."

Madison adjusted the air conditioner, then brought her grandmother a glass of iced tea.

"I hate to leave you alone, but I have some work to do. Maybe Cora can stay with you today. Just let me give her a call."

"I don't need a babysitter, Maddy, just some rest. Now quit fussing."

Twenty minutes later, Madison was driving Cora to stay with her grandmother.

"Is there anything going on that she won't talk to me about?"

"Not that I know of," Cora said, "but she's been too quiet to suit me. I'd suggested a checkup, but you know your grandmother. She won't go unless she's dying."

"I'm really worried about her. You're her best friend and she'd tell you things she wouldn't tell me. Can you think of anything we can do?"

"I have no clue what's wrong with her, but I'll pay closer attention." Cora angled the air conditioner vent to blow on her. "This heat's a bit much this soon in the season, and that doesn't help."

They were heading east on Oak Glen Road toward Bryant Street, and already the green scrub on Crafton Hills was turning brown.

"I have an idea." Cora checked her pocket calendar, flipping through the diary-size notepad and her schedule. Madison smiled at the no-nonsense sand-colored leather. No flowery covers for Cora. "Ella mentioned she'd like to take a short trip somewhere, to get away for a few days to someplace cooler. Perhaps now is the time to go."

"That's an excellent idea! I just hope you can talk her into going."

EIGHT

DEXTER PRESENTED HIS faxed request for gate clearance at San Quentin's gate and waited while the guard checked it on the computer.

The morning sun hit Dexter right in the eyes. Squinting, he tried to be patient as the moments dragged by. The year before, he'd been whisked right through, but that time he'd presented a mailed request enclosed in an official envelope. He checked the dash clock and saw that he had an hour before the hearing. He was okay—as long as there were no lengthy delays.

The guard made a phone call and Dexter ground his teeth. Was something wrong? As several more minutes passed, he feared the worst. If the fax hadn't arrived in time to generate a pass, he could miss the hearing.

He knew his testimony wouldn't prevent Bates' release if the board voted otherwise, but he had to try, had to make them understand the horror of the night that scarred Madison so terribly.

Finally, after an eternity of waiting, the pass was approved and Dexter was allowed through to the second guard station.

More than a hundred-fifty years old, the prison sprawled over four hundred acres about twenty miles north of San Francisco. It sat right on the bay, and with the palms, shrubbery, and outbuildings, including a post office, museum, and a gift shop, Dexter felt he could be in any government complex—except this one housed death row inmates and a gas chamber.

Once through the "sally port," a barred cage that's locked on both sides by floor-to-ceiling metal gates, a tall woman in her late thirties, her complexion reminding him of a rich café au lait, greeted him.

"Good morning, Detective Quinn. I'm Marsha Cummings," she offered her hand, "Victim Services Representative. I'll escort you through today's proceedings.

"I'm aware you've visited before and realize you must be familiar with the rules," she continued, "but I must reiterate Title 15, Section 3303 of the California Code of Regulations."

"The Hostage Rule."

Ms. Cummings smiled. "Just as law enforcement officials must quote the Miranda rule, we must make sure visitors know the Hostage Rule, which states, 'Employees must not permit inmates or others to use hostages to escape from custody or otherwise interfere with orderly institutional operations. Hostages will not be recognized for bargaining purposes. All inmates, visitors, and staff will be informed of this regulation.' In other words, Detective, if you're taken hostage, you're on your own."

Dexter nodded his acceptance. Nothing else he could do. He checked his watch; ten minutes until the hearing.

"We're fine, Detective," she assured him. "It's just around this corridor."

The hearing room, about fifteen-by-fifteen feet, was as tight as the one last year, but since only two other people besides Ms. Cummings and Dexter sat on the visitors' chairs lining the wall, he felt he could breathe. Recognizing the deputy district attorney from San Bernardino County as well as an assistant from the Major Crimes Unit, he nodded and took a seat. No one spoke.

A honeywood table about three-by-nine separated the visitors from the committee of two men and one woman. Files of loose papers covered the table, and steam rose from a carafe of coffee. Dexter would have liked a cup, but it wasn't offered.

Directly in front of Dexter, a lone straight chair, which he knew was for the inmate, faced the panel. Unfortunately, from his position, Dexter wouldn't be able to see Bates' face. He wanted to watch the dirtbag's expression when he told the panel about the savage slaughter that had left two dead and one woman afraid of the dark.

"Do you mind if I move to a different chair?" he asked Ms. Cummings. "I have a personal stake in the outcome, and I want to watch Bates when I testify."

After they took other seats, the door opened and two guards, one on each side of the prisoner, escorted Bates to the chair, matching the slow, shuffling steps that were all the shackles would allow. Once he was seated, the guards took standing positions directly behind him.

Dexter observed the relaxed figure, noting Bates' dark eyes scanning the parole board directly in front of him, then lowering his head in assumed repentance. But Dexter would stake his life that the dirtwad felt no such thing. Wearing jeans and a light-blue shirt with CDC PRISONER on the back, Bates appeared about the same as last year. Perhaps his mustache and beard were streaked with a little more gray, but Dexter still detected that belligerent demeanor. Bates was merely trying to hide it. At nearly six feet and dressed in black, he must have been a terrifying figure to a child.

As if feeling Dexter's stare, he raised his head and their eyes met for just an instant. He smiled slightly, an insolent smirk that Dexter wanted to wipe off his face with a fist.

"Good morning," the man in the brown suit began. With

his high cheekbones and coal-black hair, Dexter thought he might be Native American. He identified Bates by ID and case number.

"This will be a subsequent parole consideration hearing for Michael Bates," he said, then read the date Bates was received into San Quentin, "For Violation of Penal Code Section One-Eighty-Seven, causing the death of another person with malice aforethought." He gave the day's date, time, and location.

Dexter shifted in the tiny chair, impatient to get on with it.

"We'll start by establishing voice identification," the speaker continued. "I'm James Cordova, Commissioner, Board of Prison Terms." The woman and other man identified themselves as deputy commissioners, then the visitors, including Ms. Cummings, stated their names and occupations.

"The purpose today is to consider the suitability of parole for Michael Bates," Cordova said. "Mr. Bates, you have the right to present relative documents to this hearing, the right to an impartial panel. We've reviewed your file, including psychiatric reports and psychological evaluations, your work in the library, participation in group therapy, and your educational achievements, which include obtaining your GED. Congratulations."

Bates preened.

What the hell is this? Oh, Christ, Dexter thought, they're going to let him go.

"A copy of today's transcripts will be sent to you," Cordova continued, "and you have the right to appeal within ninety days. We'll begin with the offense. You are not required to admit guilt. We'll accept the court documents as fact. Do you swear to tell the truth today?"

Bates nodded.

"Please state your answer aloud."

"Yes," Bates said.

The asshole wouldn't know the truth if it hit him in the ass, Dexter thought. Why the hell didn't the state fry him when they had the chance? A lethal injection like they did now was too painless for a cold-blooded monster like Bates.

Cordova read the court's account of the Youngs' murder, reading all the known details. Bates listened with his head lowered.

"That's the statement of facts, Mr. Bates," Cordova said. "Is there anything you'd like to add?"

Bates said nothing for a long moment, then he raised his eyes. Holy shit, Dexter thought. The asshole had managed to work up tears.

"I'm so terribly sorry for what I did that night," Bates said. "I know nothing I could do will ever make it right, but all I can say is that I'm sorry. I've studied the Word of God since then, and I swear I'll never hurt another living soul as long as I live."

Dexter watched the woman's face. She's buying it, he thought incredulously. He couldn't believe it.

"Anything further?" Cordova asked Bates.

He shook his head and looked down as if humbled. "I'll just throw myself on your mercy."

"Now we'll hear from the deputy district attorney and the detective on the case."

Dexter listened as the DDA gave an account of the trial and told of Bates' hostile reactions at the defense table, which had included several outbursts of obscenities. One time he'd tackled the prosecutor and had been hustled out of the courtroom. Then it was Dexter's turn.

Inch by inch, he led the committee through the Youngs' home as if he were seeing it again.

"I'd only been on the job a year when my partner and I responded to the call. We entered the two-story house in Yucaipa and began our search. We found nothing amiss on the first floor, and cautiously, weapons drawn, we climbed the stairs. Four doors were closed upstairs and one was opened. A glow was observed under one of the closed doors, so I announced myself. There was no response.

"My partner entered the room with the open door and discovered a child's empty room. He secured the rest of the rooms, then together, we entered the room with the light.

"We found Mr. and Mrs. Young's bodies in that bedroom. A small table lamp was lit on the floor next to the bed. We called for backup and emergency services, but my partner and I knew it was too late.

"Mrs. Young's nude body was on the bed, vicious stab wounds to her chest and abdomen. Blood covered the bed and the walls. In all the years since, I've never seen so much blood."

Dexter paused a moment. No one made a sound.

"She'd been raped, repeatedly, according to the medical examiner. I believe you have a copy?"

Cordova nodded, his face expressionless. "Please continue."

"On the floor next to the bed, Mr. Young had been propped against the wall, hands tied behind his back and a gag torn from Mrs. Young's nightgown around his mouth. His throat had been savagely slashed.

"More units responded to the call and a thorough search was made of the house. A child, Madison Young, six years old, was discovered crouched in the corner of her closet, wet from her own urine, so traumatized that she couldn't speak. Later, when Miss Young was able to communicate, she said Bates was coming after her when we arrived on the premises. He escaped out a lower window, but as you know, he was apprehended by officers surrounding the home.

"Mr. Cordova and members of the committee, I realize we're not here to retry Michael Bates, although I wish we could—"

"Detective Quinn," Cordova interrupted. "Please keep your narrative to what the law allows."

"When officers tried to remove Miss Young from her closet, she screamed and backed away. She's spent eighteen of the past twenty years in therapy," he went on, "and she still has nightmares.

"This *man*, if you will, should not be released into society. Before he murdered the Youngs, he was convicted of aggravated assault, for which he only served one year.

"He's violent and poses a threat to society. Studies on recidivism find that between two-thirds and three-quarters of offenders released from prison are arrested again within three years. Mr. Bates is a convicted murderer. We cannot, in all good conscience, release this man to kill again. Miss Young, her grandmother, Mrs. Ella Osborne—who assumed care of her when she was orphaned—and the community have the right to live without fear of their lives at the hands of convicted killers such as Michael Bates. Please protect our citizens by keeping him in custody."

Cordova finished his notes. When the court recessed, everyone stood. Just before the guards hustled Bates out of the room, he threw a backward glance at Dexter. For an instant, Dexter saw a chilling, shrewd smile, and he knew for certain that Maddy was still in danger.

NINE

CRAMPED IN HIS tiny airline seat two hours after the parole board's decision, Dexter was still seething. Even after several shots of rye whiskey at the airport bar, he couldn't get Cordova's words out of his head.

"After careful deliberation and review of all the records, including psychological, educational, and work duty," Mr. Cordova said, "we, the members of the California Department of Corrections panel, have concluded that Michael Bates has demonstrated repentance and remorse for his crimes, as well as a commitment to decent behavior and a desire to contribute to society.

"While we recognize that his crimes were despicable, we believe he has successfully undergone rehabilitation while in custody.

"Therefore, parole is granted."

Parole granted. Parole granted. The words echoed in Dexter's head. How the hell was he going to tell Maddy and Ella something like that? No way could they ever feel safe with that shithole loose. The system was fucked. Citizens were fucked. Dexter wanted to hit something. Despite his size, he'd never been a man of violence, but now he wanted to feel that satisfying release when he sent something flying.

After landing at Ontario International, he snarled at the attendant, and when he pulled out of the airport in his Tahoe, he felt like ramming everyone out of the way. At the I-10 east on-ramp, he slowed, and cars behind him honked.

He lowered his window. "Fuck off, you assholes!"

This wasn't good. He was liable to kill someone in the mood he was in, so, instead of taking the freeway east to Yucaipa, he pulled into the nearest lot, a hamburger joint. He grabbed some coffee and sat down. In desperate need of a friend, he entered a special number on his cell.

As ring followed ring, disappointment washed the rage away. He sagged in his seat. It was if all the tension he'd carried in the past few days evaporated, and he felt drained.

Just as he touched the disconnect button, Pam answered.

"Well hey, stranger. What's up?"

"Oh, the same old, same old. You busy?"

"Not for you, big boy. Come on up."

Smiling for the first time in several days, he pulled back into traffic. Even driving like a sane man, it was only a few minutes until he pulled outside the gates of her Rolling Hills Drive complex.

Dexter's relationship with Pamela Evans spanned over thirty years. He and his Navy buddy had been standing in line for the roller coaster at the old Pike Amusement Park in Long Beach when Pam and a friend had come along. Soon after, they all double-dated, and he had continued to see her after his discharge and entry into the sheriff's department.

They'd discussed marriage, but he gave more to the job than to their relationship, and after breaking several dates in a row, they both knew it wouldn't work. Over the years, their relationship had evolved into one of complete compatibility. As long as neither was attached to someone else, they'd meet at her townhome, have a few drinks and dinner, perhaps take a swim, then make love until the wee hours. The next morning, each would return to their own world, Pam to the software corporate world, and Dexter to the business of chasing killers.

He had barely parked his Tahoe beside her Lexus when she flew out the door and flung her arms around him. In shorts and halter top, her auburn hair sleeked back with a bandana, she looked damned good. A sheen of sweat glistened on her tanned skin.

"Don't mind me," she said, still plastered against him. Almost as tall as Dexter, she was a perfect fit. "I've been doing some weeding in the back, and I'm all sweaty, but I'm glad to see you."

"Let's take a shower together," he suggested, heading for her back door. "After the day I've had, I could stand to feel clean." Arm in arm, they entered the house, the dark hardwood floors adding to the feeling of calm and comfort.

While Pam blended frozen lime daiquiris in the kitchen, Dexter shrugged out of his coat and unbuttoned his shirt. The family room opened from the kitchen, and Dexter took his drink and settled on an oversized easy chair he'd bought several years ago and stretched his long legs on the ottoman.

"Damn, this is heaven." He drained his drink in one gulp.

Pam, one eyebrow cocked, poured him another. "Okay, I know the pleasure of my company is to die for, but something else is going on. What's up?"

"Let me enjoy this drink and a shower first. Then we'll see what comes up." He waggled his eyebrows in a leer.

"Sounds like a plan." She grinned, and carrying her drink, reached for his hand. "Come on, let's take that shower."

After they took turns soaping each other, Dexter tenderly cupped her small breasts and bent to take a nipple in his mouth. She reached for him, and after a few more minutes of play, each so familiar with the other's body that the slightest touch was welcomed, they wound up on her bed.

CORA BACKED THE family's Mercedes out of Ella's driveway and turned west to catch the southbound freeway. Madison waved one last time, relieved that Ella had not only consented to a short trip, but had mentioned the sea breezes in San Diego. The sisters thought it would be perfect, and Ella suggested leaving immediately so they could attend the evening's last performance of the new musical at the Old Globe Theater in Balboa Park.

They had certainly picked a perfect day to travel, Madison thought, lifting her face to the sky. The early afternoon sun was warm enough to leave jackets home, yet not hot enough to need air-conditioning.

She locked the front door. Even though Ella never complained, Madison knew her grandmother had missed so much in life while taking care of her, and with Ella's health slipping lately, she'd been especially worried. San Diego was the perfect place to revitalize with its soft ocean breezes and plenty of shopping and sightseeing. And, since it was only about a two-hour drive, the ladies wouldn't arrive overtired from traveling.

Now that Ella was going to have some fun, maybe it was time she did as well. Maybe she'd call Greg and suggest dinner. She might even let him pay.

A WHILE LATER, as the gray dusk was throwing the room in shadows, Dexter and Pam lay wrapped in each other's arms. Dexter felt drained, but he also felt as if a crushing weight had shifted. He might still carry the burden, but at least now he could breathe.

"You're so damn good for me," he said, giving Pam a peck on the tip of her nose. "Why didn't we ever get married?"

"Because I wouldn't have you." Lazily, she snuggled closer.

"Ah, well, there's that. I always knew you were smart."

She nuzzled his neck and reached down.

"Might as well forget that for now," he told her regretfully. "I'm an old man and I need rest."

She laughed and sat up. "Well, *old man*, you've taken advantage of my hospitality and my body, so what are you going to do for me?"

"How about I feed you?"

She jumped off the bed and headed for the bathroom. "Last one ready has to pay the tab!"

Seated later at their favorite seafood restaurant, they shared a platter of fresh oysters on the half shell. By the time dinner arrived, a steam pot loaded with two kinds of crab, sausage, potatoes, and corn, Dexter felt ready to talk.

Attacking the shells with a vengeance, he told Pam about his trip to San Quentin.

"Why on earth would they release someone so dangerous?"

"Funding issues, overcrowding, and because the do-gooders of society think a murderer can be rehabilitated."

Cracking a long joint, he pulled it apart, and carefully peeled out a long string of crab. "Perfect," he said, dipping it in the drawn butter. He chewed slowly to savor the sweet flavor.

"You don't agree, I take it," Pam said.

He gave her a cynical look.

"But isn't it possible?"

"Anything's possible, but once someone has crossed that line of taking another life, something in their psyche is changed. I don't believe they can ever regain that certain respect for human life."

"I hope you're wrong."

"So do I, but I doubt it."

"What are you going to do now?"

"Watch him like a hawk," Dexter told her grimly,

"and if he makes one move toward Maddy or her grandmother, I'll kill the son of a bitch."

"So, WILL YOU marry me?" Greg asked over his slice of
pizza. A waiter passed their table with a tray of freshly
baked Italian bread, and in the background, a ballad by
The Three Tenors offered a touch of romance.

Madison choked and Greg handed her a glass of water
to wash down her bite of pizza.

"Are you crazy? We haven't even discussed marriage."

"Just because we haven't discussed it doesn't mean I
haven't thought about it," he told her calmly, his hazel eyes
twinkling in the soft candlelight. "I knew I wanted you the
first time I saw you. And take smaller bites."

"Oh, for heaven's sake, I know how to eat. I've been
doing it my entire life. And that's exactly why I won't get
married again. I don't want you or anyone else telling me
what to do."

"You need someone to look after you, and I'm the man
to do it." Greg took another bite of pizza. "Delicious."

Taken aback, Madison stared at him. "Why you arro-
gant, uh…"

"Macho male? Stud?" he offered. "See? You need me.
You don't even know what to call me."

"That's because my grandmother brought me up to be
a lady."

"I like Ella. I thought I'd have to soften her up, but she
surprised me. She's actually on my side. She also makes a
mean peanut butter cookie, even better than mine, so I'll
definitely hang around. If you won't marry me, maybe she
will." He pulled another slice of pizza apart and put it on
her plate. "Eat more. You've lost some weight."

After several months, Madison still didn't know what
to think about Greg. Half the time he sounded serious, and

the other half, she just didn't know. He had something, a certain old-time gentleman courtesy that she was drawn to, always walking on the outside, never forgetting to open doors for her. While several inches shorter than Dexter, he was tall enough to make her feel feminine. And, he always looked at her with a warmth that made her toes curl.

She did get lonely. But still, she wasn't ready to live with anyone and she didn't know that she ever would.

"Greg, I do like you—"

"*Like* me? Ouch, that hurts."

"I'm fond of you, more so than I've been about anyone, but I can't marry anyone right now. I have problems that are difficult to live with, to say the least."

"We all have problems. Look, I was married before too, but I learned from my mistakes. Now I put the seat down and pick up my socks. I even cook. What more could you want?"

He gave her such a charming grin that she couldn't help but smile.

"It's not that simple. I have control issues, serious ones. You'd rebel and walk out."

Greg put down his pizza. "Is that what your husband did?"

She nodded. "The thing is, I don't blame him."

"I know what happened to you when you were a child, Madison. Your grandmother told me. And I understand your fear of the dark. We can work around all your fears."

"This is all too soon. We've been out a few times but we don't even know each other."

"I know all I need to know."

"My husband thought he knew me, and I still managed to chase him away."

"I'm not your husband, Madison, but okay. We'll go one step at a time. I'll take you home tonight, then I'll call tomorrow and we'll arrange to go out again. And we'll keep going out until you feel as if you know me better. Do you like the mountains? How about a picnic at Big Bear Lake? I'll supply the food."

Later, when he walked her to her door, he took her key, unlocked the door, and pushed it open to her well-lit living room.

"See?" he said. "Lights don't bother me. I want you enough to live with them. Hell, I'd even wear one of those frilly blindfold things to bed if I could have you."

"But why? How could you want me when you don't even know me?"

"I know you, Madison. I know how courageous you are, even if you don't. Your courage, for instance, when you covered the incident at Jimmy's even though it was painful."

"Some courage. I fell apart and Dexter had to rescue me."

"Doesn't matter. You were there, doing what you felt was right. I admire that. You have warmth, Madison," he told her, his voice husky. "You try to keep it hidden, but it's there. Your devotion to your grandmother, your love for Dexter. You have passion whether you know it or not." He ran his fingers through her hair. "I love the way your hair shines in the light. It reminds me of strands of liquid gold."

Madison met his gaze and the need she saw in his eyes made her knees go weak. She found herself leaning toward him, desperately needing someone to love, someone who loved her, but did she dare?

"I love your eyes," he continued in a whisper, "flashing fire at me one minute, melting me with softness the next. And your mouth…" he trailed off as he traced her cheekbone with his forefinger and thumb, then ran down her jawline to her mouth.

Madison forgot to breathe.

Then he leaned down to kiss her, a light kiss that gently caressed her lips. "I love the taste of you," he murmured. "Makes me think of a perfect, ripe peach, ready to drown me in its sweet juices."

When he pulled her to him, Madison allowed him to hold her. To feel loved, wanted, and accepted was a powerful attraction. She wrapped her arms around him, drawing in his strength. It felt so wonderful to be held, and for one, tiny, nanosecond in time, the anxiety that she constantly lived with, eased.

"I love everything that makes you uniquely you." His voice was as soft as his lips. "Give me a chance, Madison. Give us a chance. Let me in, let me love you."

She wanted more of his kisses, wanted to touch him and wanted him to touch her, but the thought of allowing someone inside her home, of relaxing her guard even for a moment, was more than she could bear. She stiffened and pulled out of his arms.

"For God's sake, Madison. Don't do this. I love you."

"You don't understand, Greg. I'm not a complete woman, so I can't offer love. Not now, maybe not ever. If I were in any condition to love someone, it would be you. But I can't. I can't even love myself." She touched his face. "I don't think we should see each other any longer."

"But, Madison—"

"I'm sorry, Greg." Without another word, she went inside and shut the door.

Once inside, she didn't try to stem the tears, weeping until she was exhausted. Would she ever be a normal person, capable of loving someone and allowing them to love her? Her first husband hadn't thought so. She still remembered how he'd recoiled in horror at her hysterical screams when he'd failed to lock one window.

She went on her nightly routine, making sure each window and door was locked. She pulled her revolver from the nightstand and touched each bullet in the cylinder just to be sure.

When she finally fell asleep, she dreamed of dark nights and heard again the terrifying sound of her mother's screams. She saw the killer's eyes, locked on her own as she stared at him through the louvered closet door.

Heart pounding, she jerked awake and lay sleepless until the alarm rang in the morning light.

Never had she felt so alone.

TEN

On his way to the bull pen, Dexter went over his list of names to contact about Bates. Ella and Maddy were first, of course, as he wanted the news to come from him. But after a sleepless night worrying about it, he still hadn't figured out the best way to break it to them.

One thing he was certain of. They should hear about the parole together so they could support each other. Or would it be better to talk to Ella first, so the two of them could prepare Maddy?

Just how the hell do you prepare someone to face the monster from her nightmares?

Dexter had always loved the justice system, believing in it so strongly that he'd spent his adult years putting his life in danger to defend and enforce its rules. Sure, it had faults, but it was a hell of a lot better than any alternative he could think of.

But now? He was taken aback that the system, for whatever reason, would allow a fiend like Bates back on the streets. Everyone knew it sometimes happened, but he couldn't let the injustice of that prevent him from continuing to track down the perps and see that they were put away. Now he was personally involved, and it was hell, and if *he* felt that way, he could imagine Ella's and Maddy's reactions.

He had to prepare them gently, carefully, praying that the news wouldn't send Maddy back into a mental and emotional relapse.

How the hell could he do that?

He should've been a shrink instead of—

A shrink! That was it. He'd call Maddy's therapist and ask her to accompany him.

Dr. King had given every sign of being committed to helping Maddy when she had been seeing her regularly, and he had no doubt she would be willing to pick up where she had left off. Especially under the current circumstances.

She had to.

So relieved at his brilliant idea that he could've broken out in song, he checked his Blackberry's address book and punched her office number. But when he asked to speak to her, the receptionist said she was on vacation.

A vacation? She couldn't be. Not now, not when Maddy's emotional health was at stake.

"When is she due to return?"

"She's due back in five days," the receptionist told him, "but she may extend her visit."

Five days? He didn't know if he could wait that long. With the overloads in the prison system, paperwork got behind and it often took a month for an inmate to walk through the gates. But Dexter had experience with those unexpected twists of fate, and Bates could be released at any time. Dexter didn't want to risk Maddy's state of mind.

"I need to speak with her on an urgent matter. I'd like her number, please."

"Are you a patient?"

Using all the authority he could muster, Dexter identified himself, adding that it was an urgent matter involving Ella Osborne and Madison Young.

She didn't give him the doctor's number, but in her cool efficient manner, she told him she'd relay the message— and she hung up.

Dexter stared at the phone. She hung up? He wasn't through speaking.

He resisted the urge to throw the phone on the floor and then head to the nearest bar, but he was afraid of how much booze it would take to calm the frustration and panic squeezing his guts. Instead, he called Senator Stone, the one man who could commiserate with him over Bates. However, after hearing the senator's voice, he kept the conversation brief. The older man hadn't sounded well at all, and Dexter hoped he'd take advantage of his down-time and get some rest.

The mayor and Marie were also on the list, but he could delay talking to them. Captain Silva needed to know.

Wanting to talk to Silva alone, he passed by Rico's desk, but to his consternation, Silva yelled for Rico.

"He's your partner, Dex. He needs to know what's going on."

Dexter ground his teeth.

Rico strolled into the office, nodded at the captain, and sat down. He avoided Dexter's eyes.

Christ, Dexter thought, he's still wearing that wounded expression. Too bad. He might actually like the guy if he'd act like a man instead of a pussy who didn't get picked for a sports team in gym class.

Dexter ignored him and brought the captain up to speed.

Silva's mouth tightened. He shuffled some papers on his desk, then dropped them.

"Yucaipa was Bates' last known residence," Dexter said, "so he'll be released back to his so-called community. Depending on their backload, it may take a few weeks for all the paperwork to get processed. That'll give us some breathing time."

Silva sat back and eyed Dexter. "I shouldn't have to say this, and I'm hoping it won't be needed, but, Dexter, no matter what your rank is, you're first a law enforcement officer. Remember that. I know your history with Bates, and I can imagine how you must feel. But watch it. I don't need a half-crazed vigilante on my team."

"Yes, sir, I understand."

"You hear me, Dex? I have enough problems."

"Yes, sir."

Silva held Dexter's gaze for a moment. "Ah, get the hell out of here."

Dexter walked back to his desk. *Half-crazed vigilante?* Not him—not unless such action was needed.

"What's up with you and a parolee?" Rico asked, pulling out his own chair. "Sounds like something I should know."

"Maybe I'll tell you about it sometime."

Rico frowned.

"Over breakfast," Dexter added with a sigh. The things he had to do just to get a vacation.

When they were served, Rico's gaze went from his platter to the server, fixing her with a beady stare. His impression of authority, Dexter thought.

"One egg yolk is flat and hard," Rico complained, "and I asked for over easy. Please take them back and have the cook prepare them the way they were ordered."

The server took his platter, but Dexter wasn't going to wait. He spread a generous layer of strawberry jam on his toast.

"Want a piece until they bring yours?" he asked, then ignoring Rico's scowl, he dug into his breakfast.

"The toast looks overdone," Rico told the server when she appeared with his breakfast, "but I don't want to wait again."

Just to keep from punching the guy, Dexter asked him

about canvassing the area yesterday around the steakhouse. "Any luck?"

"The usual. No one saw or heard anything. If something doesn't break soon, we'll have an unsolved mystery right in town. Any ideas?"

"Maybe someone in one of those houses on the hill behind Jimmy's saw something. Worth a try, but with no leads, this case goes cold."

The words hung in the air as they finished their meals.

"What's the deal with this guy Bates?" Rico asked. "Why are you so attached? They warn us about getting too emotionally involved."

Over a refill of coffee, Dexter thought about his reply. If he were doomed to have that asshole as a partner, he should at least let him know why he felt so strongly about Bates.

"It's more than a case, Rico. Madison and her grandmother, Ella Osborne, are like family. Over the years, I've spent many evenings at Ella's kitchen table.

"At first my goal was to help them through," he went on, "but I discovered I needed them as much as they needed me. Ella comforted me through my marriage and divorce, plying me with cookies, pies, and my favorite, chicken and dumplings. I'd *help* Maddy make the dumplings, and I managed to get more flour on me than in the dough." He smiled. "And when she'd laugh, well, it was a delight. That child had been through hell, and for a while, none of us knew if she'd survive.

"And now, I'm going to have to tell them news that'll shatter the world they've managed to build."

"That's a tough break," Rico said. "I've seen her review columns, even tried a restaurant or two she recommended. That's rough, but neither woman is your responsibility."

Dexter put his fork down and let go. Otherwise, he was afraid he'd stab Rico with it.

"You have any kids, Rico?"

"A son, fourteen. Lives with his mother in San Jose."

"See him much?"

"I try to, but you know how it goes. He blames me for the divorce."

"Wouldn't you do anything and everything in your power to keep him from harm?"

"Of course."

"That's how I feel about Maddy."

"She's not a relative, though, right? I mean you're not legally responsible."

Dexter couldn't figure out the little prick. And he was supposed to trust him with his life? Soon as he could after vacation, he'd dump him, no matter how much the captain bitched.

Finishing his coffee, he picked up his cell. It had been a couple of hours since he'd left word for Dr. King and still no word.

"This is Detective Quinn again," he told the receptionist. "Dr. King has not returned my call."

"I left word, sir," she said, her voice just as detached as before. "Dr. Simmons is on call. Would you like to speak to him?"

"I'm sure he's a very capable man, but I want to speak to Dr. King. As soon as possible." Keeping his irritation in check, he left his name and number once more. Was the entire world fucked?

Next, he called Ella to see how she and Maddy were doing, to get a feel for their mood, and was switched to her voice mail. He tried her cell number. Same thing. She might be out shopping, but she usually answered her cell. He wondered if anything was wrong.

Just to make sure she was all right, he called Maddy,

who assured him that her grandmother was fine and was just taking a short trip with Cora and her sister.

Although he didn't say it, he could only hope that she'd return rested enough to survive what he had to tell her.

"WILLY BOY" MARTIN STOOD in the Arizona sun, waiting in line with a handful of other people near the food bank semi parked at a local church. By the time they opened the doors in an hour, the line would be three times longer, and there never was enough food for everyone. Willy wanted to make sure he got his share.

He took a deep drag of his cigarette and blew a heavy plume of smoke, ignoring the irritated glances of the other people in line. They didn't like it, piss on 'em. They could leave.

The fat broad in front of him turned around, but before he could tell her to go fuck herself, she smiled.

"Wonder what we'll get this time," she said, eyeing him as if he were a choice cut of steak. About as wide as she was tall, she was in her thirties and wore one of those skimpy little tops that barely covered her floppy boobs. Dimpled flesh hung over her short jean cutoffs and rippled down her heavy thighs. But hey, he never turned down a piece of ass, no matter how big, so he poured it on, paying attention and laughing inside when she smiled at him. After making a date, he lost interest in her silly chatter and she finally gave up and turned around.

The sun burned hotter and he brushed sweat from his forehead with his arm. His dingy T-shirt was soaked. Tired of standing, he plopped down on the pavement. Waiting for food was woman's work, but Shantel got called in at the diner, and if he wanted a meal and a fuck later, he had to pick up the box of food.

Man, he had a good thing going; he'd sell what he didn't

eat right out of the box. In his neighborhood, buyers didn't always have money, but they traded services, especially that little Asian broad. She really knew how to use her tongue, and it only took a few moments after stepping into the alley. He got a hard-on just thinking about it.

"Waiting's hell in this heat," a voice said.

Willy looked up and could just make out an outline of someone wearing jeans silhouetted against the afternoon sun. He shaded his eyes with his hand and couldn't tell if it was a man or woman.

"Hey, man, you a him or her? Not that I usually have a problem telling," he added with a snicker.

"You can't tell?"

Willy patted the pavement beside him. "Tell you what. Sit here and I'll feel your tits. Then I'll know." He threw out his chest. "I'm an expert on tits."

"I'll sit, but keep your hands off my boobs. Just think of me as an *it*, like in Cousin Itt from the Addams Family. You ever watch it?"

"Yeah. *Thing* was cool."

Itt sat heavily beside him and stared at him from behind huge sunglasses. Instead of something light, Itt wore one of those long-sleeved sweatshirts with the hood pulled halfway over gray hair.

"Man, you crazy? Wearing that thing in this heat?"

"Keeps the sun off me."

Willy shrugged. He didn't give a rat's ass what Itt wore.

"You have a family?" Itt asked.

"Nah. Got me a woman, though. Her bratty kid lives with us."

Itt nodded and kept looking at him. Even though Willy couldn't see Itt's eyes, he felt the stare. Shit, man, as horny as he was, he wasn't hard up enough to go for an old woman—or man.

"Let me tell you a secret," Itt said, leaning toward him. Willy wasn't sure he wanted that close, but he was willing to listen. Hell, listening never hurt nobody. When Itt cupped his ear with its hand, he waited.

"What's the secret?" he asked, getting impatient. He didn't want no one seeing him too friendly with this thing.

Itt pulled an envelope from a front pocket and showed it to him. Printed on a sheet of paper was something about some society and a time and date.

"That's today," Willy said. "That supposed to mean something to me?"

"That tells when you're going to die," Itt whispered.

Willy jerked back. Just then, he felt a sharp prick in his right side and looked down to see Itt's hand push the plunger on one of those syringes.

"What the fuck?" He swatted it away, but not before he felt liquid fire spreading through his body.

"Oh, Jesus," he moaned and tried to stand. He got to his knees but a wave of contractions doubled him over and took his breath. He tried to call for help, but he had no air left. Suddenly, his arms and legs wouldn't work. He couldn't speak. His eyes watered, and his jaw froze in a silent scream.

The thing beside him stood and dropped the syringe into its shirt pocket and hurried away. Someone screamed and the broad in front of him bent down.

Her round face was the last thing Willy Boy ever saw.

ELEVEN

Mornings in Marie's office were occasions Madison tried to avoid. The ringing phones, the constant ping of new emails from her two computers, reporters barging in with the latest emergencies, all were maddening to a quiet person with too little sleep. But Marie needed information about the vice president's trip to the Near East, and Madison was recruited to search the newswire service.

"You may have to check back a few days," the editor told her, punching numbers on her fax machine. "They've kept details under wraps."

When Marie turned away to answer her phone, Madison was ready to scream. She tried to think of reasons to escape, desperate enough to wish for a sudden appendix attack. Instead, she swallowed a couple of aspirins and tried tuning out the noise.

Inching Marie's little green stuffed frog away from the keyboard, she scanned the front page of the service before scrolling through the new releases covering everything from entertainment news to the latest hot software. She clicked on the unfiltered political news and printed all the information she could find on the vice president's upcoming trip.

Just as she was ready to log out, something she'd bypassed on another page nagged her, so she clicked back and browsed the stories until she found it:

Yuma, AZ—William "Willy Boy" Martin, 27, died today of undetermined causes while waiting in line at the food shelf on Impala Drive. A witness in line with Mr. Martin stated he was seen talking to a senior individual also in line. That person fled the scene. The coroner's investigation into the exact cause of death is ongoing.

Madison read the story a couple of times and couldn't determine what there was about it that bothered her. She would have liked to send the item to her own computer, but Marie's was the only one with a subscription to the newswire service. Instead, she hit the print button.

"I'll find out," Marie was saying into her headset. "Madison, Tom thinks there's five dialects for the Arabic language. Check on that, will you?"

Back at her desk an hour later, her headache still a dull throb, Madison scanned the story from Yuma onto her office computer and emailed it to her laptop. Something about it still nagged at her, but she didn't have time to think about it now. She was behind on her reviews, so she considered revisiting one of her favorite Thai restaurants in the area, but she was scheduled for the Japanese place in Colton the next evening and didn't want to sample two Asian meals in a row. What other restaurant could she review on short notice?

Then she remembered a neighbor asking her about a new deli that had opened a couple of days before the shooting. Perfect, she thought. She could do a fast review, write it up, and get it to Marie before the deadline.

Just as she was calling the deli manager for permission to take photographs inside the restaurant and of the food, her cell phone rang. She almost let it go to voice mail, but the ID told her it was Cora. That was odd. Why would Cora be calling her? She put the deli owner on hold, something she hated to do, and clicked to accept Cora's call.

"Is anything wrong, Cora? Is Gran all right?"

"Now don't get overly concerned, Madison, but Ella hasn't been feeling well and we're on our way home."

"I'll meet you at her doctor's."

"She refuses to seek medical help. I'd object, but I don't think it's that serious. She's weak and nauseous, but I'm sure it's one of those bugs or something she ate. She rested all day yesterday and may need to stay in a few more days. She'll feel better in her own bed. We're taking our time, so barring heavy traffic, we should be home in a couple of hours."

Madison wanted to get her grandmother's house ready, but she didn't dare postpone another review. Marie had been a tolerant editor, but Madison didn't want to push her luck. No matter what happened in a reporter's personal life, the newspaper still had to go to print each day.

At the deli twenty minutes later, Madison chatted with the owner about the quality of the cold cuts he used and dutifully made notes about his wife staying after hours to make fresh potato and macaroni salad. She complimented them on one of their specials, a soup and half sandwich meal, which came with a miniature black-and-chrome kettle that sat on the table and held two cups of homemade soup.

Madison tasted a spoonful of soup, her mind on her grandmother. How much longer until Cora made it home? If Ella was nauseous, she'd need nourishing, easily digested food, so Madison decided to buy as much soup as the deli could spare.

She snapped photos of the inside of the restaurant, the plates and salads, and also of the owners, then she thanked them and took her leave.

Once at her grandmother's house, she put the soup in the fridge and checked for juices, oatmeal, and other staples she thought would be needed over the next few days. After opening windows and turning down the bed, she walked to the front porch to check for Cora's red Mercedes, and finding it nowhere in sight, took her computer from her briefcase to do some work.

She entered the title of her review and downloaded the photos from her camera, but instead of picturing the restaurant and describing the food for her readers, she found herself listening for the car. Twenty minutes later, still no further along in her article, she heard the engine and ran to the porch and down the steps.

Cora had opened the back door to help Ella out, and when Madison saw her grandmother's face, she was so shocked that she came to an abrupt halt.

ALTHOUGH JIMMY'S STEAKHOUSE was still closed, Dexter and Rico tracked down the personnel who'd been on duty the night of the shooting and questioned them about the woman in the straw hat. The results were the same as they'd been the first night: no one knew her, no one remembered seeing her in the restaurant. Some had heard the shots but thought they were backfires from the busy boulevard.

On their way back to the bull pen, Dexter tuned out Rico's prattle and checked his phone again. Dr. King hadn't returned his call yesterday, and now it was the afternoon of the second day and he still hadn't heard from her.

He called the office. Again.

"I'm sorry, but Dr. King can't be disturbed," the receptionist said in a brisk voice. "I'll be happy to connect you to her associate."

Until then he'd been polite. Now he switched to his professional voice, the low menacing growl that intimidated the toughest gangbanger.

"What's your name, young lady?" he demanded, and

then, when she told him, "Rebecca, please tell the doctor that if I don't hear from her in the next half hour, I'll show up at the office with a subpoena."

"A subpoena?"

"Tell me, Rebecca. Is your waiting room full of patients right now?"

"Of course. She and her associate are highly respected doctors."

"I'm glad to hear that, but I have to wonder how all those patients would react to several cops bursting into the office demanding access to the records."

Rico stared at him, clearly startled, but Dexter ignored him.

"Think it would shake their faith in their doctors just a bit?" Dexter asked smoothly. "Do you, Rebecca? Then why don't you save us that trouble and get Dr. King on the line. Now." Dexter hoped she wasn't versed on legalities and able to recognize bullshit when she heard it.

"I'll see if I can reach the doctor immediately," she told him stiffly.

"Young lady, I've heard that before. A half hour, then I'll be at your door."

WHEN MADISON SAW her grandmother leaning on Cora beside the car, she couldn't believe what she was seeing. Ella's entire body sagged as if she'd aged twenty years, and her face was as white as Madison's typing paper and so translucent that Madison could see the blue veins in her cheeks and forehead. Her eyes were sunken and rimmed in red.

"Gran," Madison breathed. What in God's name had happened in just a couple of days to cause such a change?

She'd always known that in the natural order of things, Ella would pass on before her, but that was an abstract knowledge, not something she'd had to think about or face. But seeing her condition now, observing how she could barely stand on her own, forced Madison to realize that one day she'd lose the person who meant more to her than anyone else on earth. And that realization terrified her.

"I'll take care of the luggage, Cora." She put her arms around her grandmother. "You and Clara go on in and have something to drink. I'm going to take Gran to her doctor's."

"No you're not, Maddy," Ella said. "I'm home and this is where I'm going to stay."

"Now, Gran—"

"Madison, I don't feel strong enough to argue, so I want you to listen. I'm not dying. I just need some rest in my own bed. If you insist on fussing, I'll go to Cora's."

Madison glanced helplessly at Cora, who simply shrugged.

"What can I say? The woman is so obstinate that you can't reason with her."

Clara looked sharply at her sister, and Ella managed a chuckle.

"Who's calling whom obstinate?" Clara asked.

Cora ignored them all and marched up the steps to the house.

After Madison settled her grandmother in bed and brought some soup, she sat on the edge of the mattress and tried to help.

"I can feed myself, Maddy. Now don't hover."

"I'm sorry, Gran. It's just that you took care of me all those years, and now I want to care for you. I love you, you know," Madison added, her eyes filling, "and I don't know what I'd do if I lost you."

"Well, you're not going to lose me, honey, at least not today. So don't fret. I just caught something, or perhaps the shellfish we had before going to the theater didn't agree with me. But whatever it was, it'll pass. I'm already feeling better."

Her face was regaining some of its rosy color, Madison observed with relief. She'd been so terrified that she could barely breathe and only realized it when she took a good, deep breath.

She leaned down and touched her grandmother's soft cheek with her own, a gesture Ella had done many times that first year after Maddy came to live with her. How wonderfully comforting it had felt to the six-year-old who'd just lost her parents. Now the touch was more for her than for her grandmother.

"I'll let you rest now," she said, gathering the dishes. "I'll be staying here the next few days to take care of you, and if you protest, I'll hover."

"Thanks, honey. That'll be nice. Now go away so I can sleep."

Back in the kitchen, Madison fixed egg salad sandwiches while Cora made a pitcher of iced tea.

"Now tell me," she asked her grandmother's friend. "What happened?"

Just as Dexter had decided to head for Dr. King's office, sans a subpoena of course, his phone rang. It was the elusive Felicia King.

"What the hell do you mean threatening my receptionist?"

"I didn't hear back from you, so I had to do something to get your attention."

"I should file charges against you, Dexter. I don't like threats, and I certainly don't like bullies."

"Who, me?"

"Don't sound so innocent. You pulled similar stunts

in the past when you tried to pry information out of me about Madison. It didn't work then and it's not going to work now. I don't have much time, so what do you want?"

"Actually, Felicia, I need your help." He brought her up-to-date about Bates' release. "Ella and Maddy have to be told, and I'm not sure how they're going to handle it. Ella is more grounded, but Maddy still leaves all of her lights on. I'm afraid the news will send her into a relapse."

"Oh, no, Dexter," King said. "I'm so sorry this has happened. Call my associate. He's good. I picked him myself."

"I don't want your associate. Maddy's used to talking to you. Besides, you know all of her history, and an associate couldn't pick it all up from a file."

"I wish I could help, but I can't get away."

"Look. If it's the fee, I'll pay. I'll even spring for your airfare home and back again."

"I'm sorry, Dexter. I can't."

"What's so damned important that you can't leave?"

"My father is dying. He's on life support and I have to be here."

CORA AND CLARA told Madison about the enjoyable time they'd had on the way to San Diego, how they'd stopped for lunch at a delightful restaurant south of Temecula. Other than being quiet and eating very little, Ella had seemed okay.

After checking into the hotel, they'd had dinner at an oceanfront restaurant, then gone to the musical. When they took a taxi back to the hotel, Ella had told them she was feeling tired and retreated to her room. The sisters had tea and dessert in the hotel coffee shop, and when they retired to the room they shared, they found a message from Ella saying she'd been throwing up and wanted to stay in bed the next day to rest, that they should go ahead with their own plans.

The next day, Ella had the Do Not Disturb sign on her door, and not wanting to wake her if she were sleeping, the sisters had gone about their plans. The morning after that, which was today, Cora called Ella's room, and after speaking to her, decided to take her home.

"I tried to get her to the doctor's," Cora told Madison, "but you know your grandmother. And actually, she seemed to perk up a bit on our way back home. I'm sure she'll be all right now."

After the sisters left, Madison tiptoed to Ella's room and stood outside the partially opened bedroom door. When she heard her grandmother's soft snore, she gave a silent thanks and crept back to the kitchen to do some work.

In front of her laptop, her notes neatly stacked on the kitchen table, she wrote the deli review and sent it to Marie. Then she clicked on the Yuma story and read it several times. What was it that bothered her? What kept her going back to read it again and again? It was only an unexplained death, and God knows there were plenty of those in the news. So what nagged at her?

When her cell rang, she ran to grab it.

"Hi, honey," Dexter said. "Any word on when Ella will be home? I'd like to stop by when she gets back."

"Actually, Dex, she's home now, but she's resting." She explained what happened. "I'll be staying with her for a few days, so why don't you tell me and then I can let her know?"

"That's okay, Maddy," he said, and for a second, she was aware of a change in his voice. "I'd rather speak to both of you at the same time. Just let me know as soon as you feel Ella is strong enough for a visitor."

"Since when are you a visitor? You know you're welcome anytime."

"I know, but I'll let her rest today and check tomorrow. In the meantime, is there anything I can do?"

After hanging up, Madison wondered what Dexter thought important enough to want an appointment to talk to them. For as long as she could remember, he'd dropped by the hillside house for coffee and cookies in the kitchen whenever he had some spare time, sometimes bringing a pizza for the three of them to share, or simply to relax in Ella's homey kitchen.

He never talked about his job or the atrocities he'd faced over the years, and while Madison had been curious at times, she learned to recognize the tight lines around his eyes and mouth and could hear the edge in his voice. During those times, she knew that whatever he'd faced had been bad, and she'd wanted to help her grandmother soothe away the demons just as he'd helped her.

Now, no matter how he'd tried to mask it over the phone, she'd heard that edge. Taking a sip of iced tea, she wondered why he felt it was important to talk to Ella and her.

DAMN. IT was bad enough to have to tell them about Bates, but to have to do so when Ella felt unwell made it worse. Dexter wondered how long he could safely postpone talking to them.

"Wait up!" Rico yelled from across Impala Drive.

He and Rico had been knocking on doors of houses behind the steakhouse in the hope someone knew something or had seen something they didn't realize was significant. So far, they had picked up nothing. Zilch.

He checked his watch. Six-thirty. Josh Gidding had probably left for the day, but Dexter hoped he'd still be in. Like others in public service jobs, parole officials put in hours of overtime. He punched Gidding's number.

With his phone to his ear, he loosened his tie and made his way to his car. Rico trailed behind. The mercury had soared to the high nineties, and although it was starting to cool down, it was still hot enough to make an iguana happy. Good ol' Inland Empire, he thought. Winter one day and full summer the next.

Gidding's number rang and rang, and with each ring, Dexter's guts squeezed a little tighter. He finally left an urgent message on voice mail. Once inside his Tahoe, he turned on the air and aimed the vents for his face. He was getting too old for this shit.

Christ! Couldn't one damned thing go right? He yanked off his tie and unbuttoned the top two buttons of his shirt.

He glanced at the sandy-brown hills surrounding Yucaipa and longed to escape to a campfire near a river. Maybe it was age, perhaps it was burnout after a lifetime of dead bodies, grieving families, and the fucked-up justice system, but with each day, the longing grew to hear the sound of water rushing over rocks or down a waterfall. Instead of sirens, he wanted to listen to the wind rustling through leaves on a shade tree and feel a cooling rain on his face.

Why the hell didn't he retire to a nice, rural state where everything was green, a place where he could sit under trees and throw a casting line into a river?

Hell. It had been years since he'd even seen a river, much less camp near one, but that was going to change. Less than two weeks and he was out of here. Only one thing could stop him, and that was Bates in his town, walking the same streets as Maddy and Ella.

Rico opened the passenger door and slid in.

"¡Válgame Dios!" He wiped sweat from his face. "This is brutal. How about we knock off for something cold to drink?"

"Best suggestion you've made all day."

When Rico headed for the men's room at Denny's, Dexter made an appointment with the mayor for the next morning. They'd need to call a special city council meeting to alert the city that a parolee with a violent history was about to be released into its midst. Since there was no official word on the exact date Bates would be released, Dexter didn't want to delay too long.

He'd also talk to Marie, let her know what he was planning. As editor of the local newspaper, and especially considering her involvement in the community, she deserved to know.

He knew he should clear all of this with the captain, but he didn't want to risk Silva nixing the idea. Bates might not be released for another few weeks, but he didn't want to risk waiting. Fate had already thrown one of those fancy twists that put the screws to everyone's lives, and if another happened, he was damned well going to be prepared.

When he called Marie, the only off-time she had available was that evening, so, trusting that she had enough decency to hold the story until he'd had the chance to talk to Maddy and Ella, he decided to go ahead and meet her.

He just hoped Ella would be strong enough the next day to hear the news.

TWELVE

JERICHO ONE STOOD at the carved wooden door, ready to welcome each Society member with a handshake before leading them to the table and encouraging them to help themselves.

Instead of the usual tray of fruits, pastries, and finger foods, the sideboard held iced platters of crab legs, shrimp, and oysters on the half shell. Delicate glass side dishes held lemon quarters and seafood sauce. For the two members who didn't care for seafood, a platter held halved sourdough loaves topped with reddish-rare prime rib slices. Cantaloupe quarters held chunks of mango, papaya, and kiwi, and two carafes, one for water and the other for wine, stood in the center of the table between the two lamps. A coffee carafe stood by Number Three's place.

When all six had arrived, Jericho selected a few food items from the buffet, took the chair at the head of the table, and chatted amicably with the members.

After the table had been cleared, Jericho began the meeting.

"Thank you all for attending this emergency session. I know some of you have traveled a great distance, especially you, Number Five, but I'm sure you're aware that I wouldn't have called this meeting if it were not urgent." After a pause, the chairperson continued.

"A situation has arisen and intervention is immediately needed." Jericho handed two sheets of paper clipped together to each member.

"Michael Bates, forty-seven, Caucasian, from Yucaipa, California, was convicted twenty years ago for the torture and murder of Mr. and Mrs. Daniel Young, also of Yucaipa. A daughter, Madison, age six, was in the home, and after Bates brutally murdered her parents, he entered her room as well. He testified at trial that he'd intended on 'getting her too,' but fled when he heard police sirens."

Jericho recounted in detail the acts Bates had committed on the Youngs, then passed glossy photos of the two victims, of the six-year-old child, and of Michael Bates at the time of conviction and also one taken at his last parole hearing.

"He was sentenced to execution at San Quentin, but Bates got lucky. The courts were arguing that execution was unconstitutional, and a temporary moratorium on capital punishment was enforced. Bates' execution was converted to a life sentence. And because of that life sentence, he's been eligible for parole and has, indeed, been before the board several times. Fortunately, the request has been denied—until the last hearing. Mr. Bates will be released as soon as the paperwork can be completed." Jericho paused to take a sip of water.

"I think you'll agree, after reading his history," the chairperson continued, "not only would his execution have saved the tax-paying citizens the expense of his care, but it would have eliminated the threat to those still living. He's an imminent danger not only to the community to which he'll return, but to the lives of the remaining family he brutally slaughtered.

"Mrs. Young's mother, Mrs. Ella Osborne, still resides in California as does Miss Young, who was severely traumatized and, judging from psychiatric records, still carries emotional scars," Jericho explained. "But the reason for this intervention is that during his trial, Bates vowed to return for the daughter. It may have been a blusterous threat, but the petitioning member does not want to take that risk."

Several members studied the photos as if to reinforce the necessity of their proposed actions.

"The requirements for the execution have been met," Jericho went on. "All that's needed is your approval."

As was the custom, the ruby bowl was passed somberly around the room for each member's vote. After they were counted, Jericho announced the decision.

"So WHAT'S UP?" Marie asked, scooping salsa onto a tortilla chip. She'd changed from her usual pantsuit into a sleeveless blouse over linen trousers and her hair was swept back into a French braid.

Dexter sat across from her in a Mexican place in Mentone, a small hillside community near Yucaipa. He swirled the crushed ice in his margarita glass, trying to decide how much to tell her. While he knew of her impeccable character, he also knew she was a devoted newspaper editor.

"Can I trust you not to print the information I'm about to give you? At least not yet?"

"Sounds ominous."

"You haven't answered my question."

"How can you ask me something like that? The people are entitled—"

"Don't hand me that shit. I want an answer. Not from the newspaper, but from you. Otherwise, this meeting is over."

"Why such hardball?" Then, when stony silence was his response, "At least tell me why I can't print it, then I'll give you my answer." Marie took another handful of chips and washed them down with a swallow of her drink.

"I don't want the two people personally affected to read about it before I have a chance to talk to them. And I can't talk to them until tomorrow, or possibly the day after."

"You must think a lot of them to feel so strongly."

"I do." Such a simple answer, Dexter thought, to express twenty years of feelings for the Young family. "Look. All I'm asking for is a couple of days. And I don't have to tell you anything. You can find out at the special city council meeting just like everyone else."

"I'm not aware that a council meeting's been scheduled."

"It will be."

Marie eyed him for a long moment. "So why tell me now?" she asked.

"Because of our long association."

A skeptical look crossed Marie's face.

"And there's always the risk you'll find out and print it before I'm ready," he added.

"I've worked with you on committees and other volunteer projects over a lot of years," Marie said, "and it doesn't take much deduction to know how important Ella and Madison are to you. And something this serious must mean news about Bates."

Dexter was taken aback. He'd almost forgotten how good she was at her job, how she made it her business to know the important things about the community and her employees.

"Close your mouth, Dexter. You don't want to catch flies."

He grinned. "You never cease to amaze me." He told her about the trip to San Quentin and the board's decision. "Ella's been ill, so I haven't been able to break the news to them yet."

"Nothing serious, I hope."

"I don't think so or Maddy would have her at the hospital."

When their food came, they dug into fish tacos with cabbage and fresh cilantro, and chiles rellenos with beans and Spanish rice as accompaniments. One thing about it, Dexter thought. He might hate the heat in the Yucaipa Valley, but the area had damned good food.

Marie stirred her drink. "I can't believe they'd free Bates, not after what he did. I'd hoped they would've fried his ass."

Dexter's eyebrows climbed. "Such language. I'm surprised."

"Can it, Dexter. We have to do something. That piece of shit shouldn't be allowed in our community."

"We can't stop it, Marie. You know that."

"We'll see."

AFTER DINNER, MADISON SETTLED her grandmother on the sofa with the TV remote in her hand, then she set her laptop on the coffee table.

Although Ella claimed she felt stronger, watching her declining health caused Madison to realize what had caught her eye about the Yuma and Yucaipa articles.

She read the article once more, then pulled up her notes on the Yucaipa shooting. Middleton, the man she'd interviewed, had mentioned an older woman with Hawley.

In the Yuma story, she highlighted the word "senior" and sat back and compared the two stories. There it was. Two sudden deaths with references to senior citizens.

Could there be a connection? A sudden image of a gun-toting old lady going around shooting people popped into her head, and she dismissed it as absurd. Besides, the first shooting had been in Yucaipa, California, and the other death, which the police hadn't even called a murder, had been in Arizona.

She ran several searches on her computer, looking for unexplained deaths or murders with the word "senior" or "senior citizen" included. What came up was disappointing. Page after page of articles including items about senior officers, senior relatives, senior advisors, and even one about a short story as a senior thesis. Not at all what she wanted.

As much as she dreaded entering the den of fire, she'd ask Marie's permission to run the newswire service. She didn't know why this nagged at her, and normally she'd avoid anything with violence. Perhaps working in a newspaper office had taught her to instinctively know when something felt amiss.

Two hours later, after settling Ella in bed and checking each door and window, she found a comfortable spot on the pillow and closed her eyes—but only for a moment. Her gaze swept her old room, the light from her bedside lamp brightly illuminating every corner, and she could see the light from the hallway, also on as well. Maybe it was time she grew up and started living like a normal person.

Determined to give it a try, she reached for the knob on her pink hurricane lamp, the same one she'd had as a child, and switched it off.

There. She'd done it. It wasn't so bad.

Instead of inspecting the dark room again, she firmly closed her eyes.

From outside her darkened window, behind the ruffled curtains and closed shutters, she heard a slight rustling sound. She tensed, but told herself that everything was okay, that she was safe in her grandmother's home.

She closed her eyes again, but instead of relaxing, she listened for the next sound, hoping, praying she wouldn't hear it.

Just as she began to relax, she heard it again, that same sound, only slighter louder.

She sat up. Was there a breeze tonight? She didn't remember noticing one before. Please God, let there be a breeze. She crept to her door to listen, and heard something that sounded like shingles rattling on the roof.

Except that shingles didn't rattle, even in a strong breeze. Or did they?

She didn't know how long she stood, alert to any noise she couldn't immediately identify, but after hearing nothing more, she crept back to bed. The wall sconce in the hallway was still lit, a habit her grandmother had begun when Madison first came to live with her. The yellow light spilled into her room and illuminated her doorway, so if she kept her eyes on it, she would see a shadow if someone were moving toward her room.

Her eyelids felt heavy. She needed rest, needed to wake in the morning strong enough to care for her grandmother. Watching her doorway all night wouldn't help either of them, but how could she relax enough to fall asleep?

Then she remembered how she'd loved to draw, the one way she could relax and forget everything. Digging in her closet, she pulled out the box holding her artist supplies, items she hadn't used in years.

In bed moments later, surrounded by her sketch pads, spiral notebooks, crayons, and charcoal sticks, she began her charcoal strokes, thinking about Greg, wondering if she could replicate the way his eyes softened when he looked at her.

A half hour later, she stared at the sketch she'd drawn, so horrified that she shoved all the supplies onto the floor.

Before her was Michael Bates, his piercing eyes staring at her from the sketch pad.

THIRTEEN

A LITTLE BRIBERY never hurt, Madison thought, entering the office carrying Marie's favorite breakfast, a dish of hot cinnamon rolls smothered with cream cheese frosting. All heads turned as the spicy, sweet aroma wafted through the office. Luckily, she'd brought enough for everyone or she'd be tarred, feathered, and run out of town.

"Marie in?"

"Give me one first, then I'll spill," Sue said.

Madison laughed. "I promise I'll save you one, but Marie gets first pick."

She'd set the alarm an hour early and had popped the rolls into the oven while fixing breakfast for her grandmother.

Thank goodness Ella was looking more like herself. A sure sign that she was feeling better was bossing Madison in the kitchen and refusing to be pampered. Madison was so relieved by her grandmother's recovery that she felt more lighthearted than she had in years.

Marie was bent over her PC. Good, Madison thought, the Mac was free.

As soon as Madison entered the room, Marie sniffed the air. "Cinnamon rolls. Okay, what do you want? My prized pooch? My five-year-old car? Whatever it is, you got it." She jumped up, took a couple of paper plates and plastic cutlery from a file drawer, and helped herself to a roll.

"What else do you have in those drawers?" Madison asked.

"Top secret stuff that I'll never tell. So what's up? You didn't go to all that trouble just to see me smile." She licked a dab of frosting from her finger and sighed in ecstasy.

"I'd like to use the wire service and do a search for any stories that might tie in with these," Madison said, handing the articles and notes from her briefcase.

Marie glanced at the notes and helped herself to another roll.

"These what, Madison? I don't see anything relevant."

"It may not be much, but I'd like to check them out. Look. Both stories are about someone dying, and in each, there's mention of a senior near them before they died."

"So? According to statistics, there are over thirty-six million seniors in the country."

"But read the articles. One's a murder and the other is an unexplained death of a man in his twenties. Don't you find that strange? Let me do some research, see if I can find any other stories like that. You're always talking about training me to be a news reporter, so now I'm interested."

Marie put down her plate and slowly, carefully, wiped her hands on a paper towel.

Madison knew her editor well enough to recognize the signs of disinterest. Only then did she realize how important it was for her to investigate.

"I don't have the time to train you right now and frankly," Marie said, not meeting her eyes, "I don't see a story here. You're wasting your time. Besides, I'm using the computer."

"What if I do it on my own time? I plan on checking on Gran at lunch, and I have the review at the Japanese place this afternoon, but I could work it in. I could come in after hours, do some checking on my own."

"You know the publisher doesn't approve overtime."

"Marie, this would be on my own time. What's the problem?"

"Our insurance doesn't cover anyone after office hours."

That didn't sound right to Madison. She'd heard Marie talk several times about the late evenings she'd spent putting the paper "to bed," but since she wasn't familiar with business insurances, she didn't argue. Besides, she could see her editor's lips tighten and knew it was time to drop the subject.

"I hope Ella's feeling better." Marie handed the dish of rolls to Madison. "Thanks for bringing them in. Just pass the rest around the office," she added, dismissing Madison by turning to her PC.

Madison stood like a statue holding the dumb rolls, watching Marie ignore her, trying to understand what had just happened.

"Marie—"

The ringing phone interrupted, and Marie's relief was obvious. She grabbed it and again turned her back to Madison.

Madison waited a few moments, hoping Marie would finish her conversation and get back to her so they could talk, but as soon as Marie hung up, she rushed out of her office to talk to Sue. She said nothing more to Madison, didn't even glance her way when Madison walked back to her desk.

It didn't make sense. Madison had never known Marie to discourage any of her staff from investigative reporting. On the contrary, she'd always welcomed it. And, she hadn't been using the Mac; she'd been at her PC instead.

Madison left Marie's office feeling as if she'd been rudely dismissed, and she had no idea why.

THE CONFERENCE ROOM in Yucaipa's city hall was as familiar to Dexter as his own squad room. The Honorable Walt
Goodman had always been active in city affairs, attending
as many Yucaipa functions as he could, believing city government should personally be involved in its community.
He'd attended Little League games as well as the opening
of new businesses, and he, Marie, and Dexter had spent
many evenings drafting new incentives and scholarships
for the city's youths.

Today, Dexter had the unpleasant duty of having to tell
the mayor about the threat to his city.

"Thanks for seeing me on short notice." He shook hands
with his friend. At nearly seventy, Goodman stood as tall
as he had in his younger days. His military posture was
softened slightly by his thick white hair.

"It sounded urgent, Dexter. Come, sit down, have a cup
of coffee." The mayor led the way to a highly polished conference table. But the true focal point of the room was the
view through the wide bay windows of the city. As before,
Dexter took a moment to gaze at the city from the bluff on
which the city hall had been built.

His community, his adopted home.

He'd watched Yucaipa grow from a quiet little town full
of orange groves to a thriving community with a population of over fifty thousand. Nestled in the foothills of the
San Bernardino National Forest about seventy-five miles
east of Los Angeles, the city maintained its hometown
atmosphere. Citizens were involved in city government
as well as with community events. Each Fourth of July,
the city celebrated at the high school stadium with bands,
games, fireworks, and flyovers from March Air Reserve
Base. The Elks, the Moose, and the American Legion held
lunches, dinners, and other events open to the public. Even
in the near-desert heat, the recreational areas flourished,

and people flocked to the regional park or to one of the several golf courses. A top-ranking community college overlooked the city from the top of a foothill. Gang activity was almost nonexistent and the overall crime rate was low. The shooting at Jimmy's was an anomaly. Citizens felt safe, which was the way Dexter wanted to keep it.

Goodman poured coffee into two mugs and took them to stand next to Dexter. They sipped in companionable silence and gazed over the city they each loved.

"We have a problem," Dexter said.

MADISON SPENT THE rest of the morning working on her outline for the review scheduled that afternoon, making notes on the items she wanted to cover, but she had trouble concentrating. Several times Marie had walked past her without speaking or even glancing her way. Madison replayed the morning several times, but she still had no idea what had happened. Or why.

The morning's bright spot had been her call to her grandmother. She'd planned to stop by the drugstore for camera batteries, then pick up sandwiches for the both of them. But when she called, she was astonished to learn Ella had lunch waiting for the two of them.

Madison's favorite tuna salad recipe with chopped apples spread between Ella's homemade bread and green salad was an unexpected treat. The table was set, and Madison poured iced tea.

"I thought about setting up the patio table on the porch," Ella told her, "but it got too hot even for me."

"This is wonderful, Gran, but you shouldn't do too much. You need rest to get your strength back."

"I know my limits, so don't think you can mother me. I'm too old for that. Besides, I need to keep busy and you know cooking is my pleasure. Now eat your lunch like a good girl and let me enjoy myself."

Madison grinned and gave Ella a kiss on the cheek. Now that she knew her grandmother was okay, relief fueled her appetite and she realized she hadn't eaten more than a nibble for several days.

However, Ella only picked at her food.

"I don't want anything heavy in my stomach," she said. "Don't worry, I'll be just fine."

But she didn't seem fine. Now that Madison had finished her lunch, she noticed that Ella was continually checking the wall clock over the door and rearranging the silverware. If Madison hadn't known better, she'd say her grandmother was fidgeting, something she never did. Perhaps she was on new medication, but Madison didn't remember a recent trip to the doctor. Ella didn't tell her everything, she knew, and now that she was getting older, and especially after how she'd looked yesterday, Madison vowed to keep better watch over her.

She'd planned to discuss what had happened with Marie, but now she hesitated. Not only did her grandmother seem a little unsettled, but she'd worked with Marie on community projects for years, and Madison didn't want to put her editor in an unfavorable light. She knew how loyal Ella was, and even though she considered Marie a friend, Madison came first. Always.

"Cora's coming over this afternoon," Ella said. "She's taking me to the cemetery. Would you like to go?"

"You know I have that review this afternoon."

Ella said nothing for a few moments, then took Maddy's hand.

"Honey, your parents' death wasn't your fault. I hope one day you realize that."

"I know." Maddy automatically patted Ella's hand, then grew quiet.

"What is it?"

"I don't remember her, Gran. Even though I was only six, I should remember something. I can see my dad's face, I remember him throwing me in the air and catching me, but I don't remember my mother."

Ella rose and gave Madison a hug.

"You will, honey, when you can forgive yourself."

Madison blinked back tears. "Now, about you," she briskly said, determined to shove her guilt to the side. "Do you really think you should go out today?"

After a long look at Madison, Ella took her seat. "I'll enjoy the outing. Besides, Cora's almost as bad as you. She won't be satisfied until she sees that I'm not on my deathbed." She opened her half-sandwich, took a small bite of the tuna, then put her fork down.

"Gran," Madison, said, wanting to phrase it delicately, "are you, by any chance, taking any new medications?"

"Of course not. Why would you ask?"

"Just wondering. You seem a bit…anxious."

"Maybe I'm feeling cooped up. You know I like to get out and walk, and with the trip and all, I haven't had any exercise for a week."

Madison hoped that was all it was. "Would you like something from the sushi restaurant?"

"Are you kidding? I might be willing to try new things, but raw fish isn't one of them. Back when your grandfather was alive and we all went fishing, we used that stuff for bait."

Madison laughed. What great times they'd had, going up the mountain to Big Bear. She missed them and decided, just as soon as Ella felt a little stronger, to take her up to the lake for a picnic. It would be good for both of them.

When the wall phone rang, Madison wondered if it were Dexter. As highly as she thought of him, she hoped he'd wait another day or two to talk to them. He hadn't sounded as if he had good news and she wanted Ella to have another day's rest.

The conversation only took a few minutes.

"That was the senator checking up on me," Ella told her. "He wanted to let us know about a garden party he's hosting in a couple of weeks. How very fortunate I am to have him as a friend."

But the look in her eyes told Madison that she was thinking of something else entirely.

AFTERNOON TRAFFIC ON I-10 west was so light that Madison made excellent time covering the eighteen miles to Colton, a neighboring city rich in Old West history.

Originally a railroad town laid out in the late eighteen-hundreds when the Southern Pacific Railway moved eastward from Los Angeles, it had been home to the Earp family. Nicholas P. Earp, father of the Earp brothers, had owned a saloon, and Virgil Earp had been the town's first marshal. It also had a large slice of the region's citrus industry, which, by the late eighteen-hundreds, could boast half a million citrus trees, most of which, today, had been replaced by light industry and single-family homes. Colton was one of the fastest growing regions in the Inland Empire.

It also housed one of Madison's favorite Japanese restaurants. Today, though, she was going to bypass the grill tables in favor of sushi for her readers.

She made her way past the outside gardens, and once inside, instead of taking the walkway to the teppanyaki tables—teppan was Japanese for iron plate, she'd learned, and yaki meant grilled—she took a seat at the S-curved sushi bar in the back. Then, while three chefs performed their magic for appreciative customers, Madison took photos and notes.

The manager suggested a spicy tuna roll topped with avocado and a spicy sauce, which turned out to be her favorite, and she also ordered a dish of sushi, rice in finger shapes topped with filets of raw fish—red tuna, salmon, which was orange with white marbling, and pink yellowtail. Madison thought she'd try chopsticks, but she dropped everything and soon went back to her fork. No wonder the Japanese were slim people.

One of the ladies in a group of three seniors kept watching Madison take photographs and make notes, and after about a half hour, the woman finally came over and introduced herself.

"My family and I enjoy your columns, Miss Young," she said, "and we always look forward to your next one. I was just telling my friend Grace that I've run into newspaper people several times the past couple of weeks."

"Oh?" Madison said politely. Ready to leave, she was packing her equipment and only half-listening.

"I stopped by that little lounge on Kipling Avenue the night of that terrible murder," the woman prattled on, "not that I frequent bars, you understand, but—"

Madison tuned out the rest of the woman's chatter. Maybe she'd stop at the market and pick up some of Ella's favorite ice cream.

"—saw your editor there."

"What? You saw my editor the night of the murder? I think you're mistaken. She was working on a story out of town."

"It was your editor, all right," the woman assured her. "I've seen her often enough at town meetings to know her anywhere. It must've been right after the shooting, because we could hear the sirens from inside. She was washing her face in the bathroom and fixing her hair. I even spoke to her, but I didn't let on that I recognized her. You know how some people are, they don't want to be seen in bars."

FOURTEEN

CAPTAIN SILVA SIFTED through a stacked pile of manila envelopes on his desk. "Time to move on. Too many other cases stacking up."

"I'd agree, but something doesn't add up." Dexter sat in the cramped chair, his long legs sprawled in front of him. "I haven't located the woman in the straw hat, and she's important to the case."

"You've canvassed the area, checked leads, and you still have nothing. Hell, the woman could've been a passerby."

"He's right," Rico piped up. He sat so stiffly in the other chair that Dexter thought he could've had a rod stuck up his ass.

"Shut up, Rico."

"Tish and Chris have their hands full," Silva went on, ignoring the exchange between the two detectives. "Frank's appendix finally landed him in the hospital, Bob's still on vacation, and I need the manpower."

Although the number of homicides in San Bernardino County had been falling for the past couple of years, some asshole, rage fueled by the summer heat, always shot, stabbed, or beat someone else to death. A large percentage of the murders were gang-related, but with a population of over two-million people, there were other cases just as senseless. Robberies gone wrong and domestic violence were year-round events.

"Mayor Goodman just alerted me about the special city council meeting he's calling." Silva said. "You'll be there?"

"If he gets it done before I leave," Dexter told him. "Eight days and counting."

"Your project, you be there."

"What project?" Rico asked.

Silva eyed Dexter wearily. "You didn't mention it to him?"

Dexter shrugged.

"What's going on?" Clearly puzzled, Rico looked back and forth between them.

"Better explain it to your partner."

Dexter skimmed through an explanation.

"All this is going down and you didn't bother to tell me?" Splotches of red dotted Rico's face. "We're supposed to be partners."

"We are partners, but we're not joined at the hip. Besides, it's old business."

"If it's going on now," Rico told him, "it's new business. And if it involves you, I need to know."

Christ. As much as he hated to, Dexter had to hand it to Rico on that one.

MADISON FELT SHAKEN. Marie at a bar in Yucaipa rather than in Long Beach? It didn't make sense. All the way back to the office, Madison kept hearing the woman's words. Surely she was mistaken.

But she'd sounded so positive that Madison had no choice but to believe her.

Rush hour on I-10 was slowing everyone to a crawl, so she was glad she was close to the Yucaipa exit. She took the off-ramp and glanced at the gas station, but the islands were crowded and it was still too hot to wait in the sun. She headed up the boulevard toward the office.

Why would Marie lie? And especially that night. The woman said Marie had been washing her face and fixing her hair. Fixing her hair could be explained; many women touched up their makeup and hair while in the ladies' room. But washing her face?

Then a horrible thought slammed her. Could Marie have been the mysterious woman with Hawley the night he'd died?

But no, she couldn't be the one. Middleton had said that it had been an older woman. Even though in her late forties, Marie would never be classified as an older woman.

Or would she?

Madison had heard Dexter voice his frustrations about the justice system enough to know that, contrary to popular belief, witness testimony was often far from accurate. Perception, memory, and the witness's own bias always came into play. And Middleton had admitted he hadn't seen the woman; he'd just heard Mr. Searl mention her to the deputy.

So it was possible that Marie had been that woman. But if she had been, why had she been with Hawley? They certainly weren't friends going to dinner together.

Madison needed some time to gather her composure, so she pulled into Jimmy's parking lot. The yellow tape was still there, the only sign that an investigation was in progress.

She walked to the area where she'd been standing the night of the murder, hoping that by some miracle, she'd realize that her suspicions of Marie's involvement were ridiculous. However, after a few moments of feeling nothing but the ninety-degree heat, Madison got back into her car, no closer to answers than she'd been before.

A few irritated honks from behind alerted her to her absentminded crawl on Yucaipa Boulevard, no doubt due to her reluctance to go back to the office.

What should she do with this new information? Should

she mention it to Marie? Even if she tried to sound casual, Marie would surely take offense. If things were awkward now, that would wipe out any chance of restoring their friendship—and, Madison realized, perhaps her job as well. How could she work in an environment where she'd accused her boss of lying?

She could tell Dexter, of course. He'd laugh at her wild imagination and convince her she was way off base.

At least she hoped that was what he'd do.

She picked up her cell phone, deciding there was only one way to find out.

"How about if I stop by Ella's this evening?" Dexter suggested, his long legs spread in front of his desk chair. "I still want to talk to the both of you, so it'll be a good opportunity to discuss your concerns as well as mine."

"No!" Maddy almost shouted over the phone. "I don't want Gran to hear this."

"Is it her health?"

"It's nothing to do with her. Please, Dex, I need to talk to you now, or as soon as possible."

Dexter had never heard that sense of urgency in Maddy's voice. Had she found out about Bates from someone? But no, she'd said it had nothing to do with Ella. And no one else, at least anyone who knew the family, had information about his release.

So what else could it be?

He rose, took his jacket from the back of his desk chair, and slipped it on. Rico looked up.

"What's up?"

"Gotta see a man about a horse." Christ, Dexter thought immediately afterward. He swore he'd never use that phrase, the one his father had always used when he'd wanted to give his son the slip. He'd leave the house and disappear for days before finally disappearing for good. Dexter had been nine and he hadn't seen him since.

Rico sprang from his chair. "Saddle it up for two, because you're not leaving without me."

Dexter grinned. Strike another one for the little prig. It might be interesting to see how enthusiastic he was when he found out what he was getting himself into.

THE COFFEE SHOP east of Calimesa off I-10 was known for its fast and cheap family meals. Easy to clean orange vinyl booths lined the walls and small tables stood in the center. Plastic potted plants in plastic tubs were scattered about and Country and Western music played softly in the background. Dexter spotted Maddy in a back booth behind one of the potted plants.

"Kind of 'cloak and dagger' stuff, isn't it?" He teased.

She smiled briefly, but seemed taken aback at Rico's presence. After introductions were made and they took a seat opposite of her, she went quiet.

"My," Rico said, leaning toward Madison, "you're even prettier than the photo with your column, which, by the way, I always enjoy reading."

Madison actually blushed, and Dexter felt as proud as if he were directly responsible.

"Thank you." She kept her gaze down and said nothing more.

A teenage boy bussed the table next to them. Dishes and utensils clattered. Even the cleaning fluid spray sounded loud.

"How's your grandmother?" Dexter asked to get her talking. He doubted she'd asked to meet him to discuss the weather.

"She's much better. She rested most of yesterday and it seemed to do her good. She was even going to do a little shopping with Cora today." Her gaze went to Rico and she grew quiet again.

"How about giving us some time alone?" Dexter told him. He jerked his head toward an empty booth across the room.

"Dex—"

"It's personal, Rico."

But even after Rico stomped to another booth, Madison still couldn't get the words out.

"What is it, Maddy? What's so difficult for you to talk about?"

"It's Marie, Dex. Now that you're here, I don't know how to begin. I feel as if I'm betraying someone who has done nothing but help me, and I'm not even sure there's cause. You'll probably think I'm being silly."

"Why don't you let me decide? Start at the beginning and tell me what happened."

She started talking, hesitantly at first, telling him how something she'd read in the newswire stories had bothered her and how, at her grandmother's, she'd realized what it was. She related asking Marie permission to use the newswire service and her editor's strange reaction.

Dexter listened patiently, relieved to hear it was nothing serious. He was sure Marie had simply doubted the wisdom of letting Maddy get involved in a story when Bates was due to be released.

But since he hadn't told Maddy about Bates, he couldn't tell her why Marie behaved as she had.

So he simply listened.

"Then that woman said she saw Marie the night of the murders. Here in Yucaipa, Dex. Can you imagine? Marie told me she was in Long Beach, so why would she lie? And why would she have been washing her face? Women don't usually do that in a public restroom."

"Wait a minute," Dexter said, leaning toward Maddy. "This woman said she saw Marie in Yucaipa? Was she sure it was Marie? She could've been wrong. Happens all the time."

"That's what I thought, but I questioned her. Discreetly, of course, and she recognized her from town meetings. There's no question, Dex. It was Marie."

Dexter sat back. That threw him. He could explain Marie's reaction to Maddy getting involved in a story, but not why she lied about being in Yucaipa the night of the murder. If it had been any other reporter assigned to the story, Dexter wouldn't have thought anything of it, but Marie knew about Maddy's aversion to violence, knew the trauma she still experienced as a result from what happened that night years ago. Marie was too good a person to put Madison on the scene unless something else was going on.

Just what could've been so important that she'd risk Madison's emotional health?

FIFTEEN

EXCEPT FOR AN occasional surly look at Dexter, Rico stared silently out the passenger window all the way back to the bull pen. Dexter managed to ignore him until he sighed, a loud, contrived sound that conjured up images of Dexter's ex-wife when he'd missed dinner, a party, or had worked until the wee hours of the morning. Sometimes it had seemed that he never stopped cajoling her out of her exasperation or apologizing for doing what was, after all, his job. Now, by God, he didn't have to apologize to anyone. Certainly not to the prick next to him.

"All right," he said, pulling into the parking lot. He shut off the engine. "Spill it."

Rico's mouth set into a rigid, thin line.

Dexter waited, but the late afternoon sun beat through the windshield and it was too damned hot to sit long. Finally, just as he grabbed the handle to open the door, Rico spoke.

"Just what is it going to take for you to accept me as your partner?"

Ah, Christ-all-Friday. On the rare occasions when Dexter felt lonely enough to consider marrying again, all he had to do was think of that tone in his wife's voice. He didn't blame her for wanting a husband home each night, but he was a cop who loved his job, and as long as he continued his career, nothing, certainly not her disapproval, could interfere with his dedication.

And now, instead of a wife, he had a partner. While he resented Rico's intrusion, he could understand his reaction.

A partnership in law enforcement was like a marriage. Two people spent the major part of each day working and eating together, making life decisions together—only instead of taking the hours, days, or months to come to a decision that a normal couple contemplating a future might make, life decisions on the job were often instantaneous, made with the knowledge that the decision could eliminate your future.

Do you follow your instincts, and, weapons drawn, rush the perp, or do you first consider the danger to each and every face in the crowd? Do you take aim when a perp points a gun at a bystander's head and uses him as a shield, or do you try to talk him down? Which partner kicks down the door during a nanosecond's lull in gunfire and enters the perp's residence? Life decisions, decisions that have to be made in an instant. And during that instant, you'd better know your partner will cover your back.

Was he sure Rico would cover his?

What was it about Rico, he wondered, that irritated the hell out of him? He was a self-righteous asshole, but what the hell, everyone had their faults, and Dexter had adjusted to several partners during his long career.

Was it the way Rico dressed? Instead of yanking something off the rack like the other detectives, Rico wore finely tailored pin-striped suits in dark colors with shirts a shade or two lighter. Today he wore a charcoal suit with a dark gray shirt and an iron-gray tie, an outfit that made him look like a pit boss for the syndicate.

"Why do you wear clothes like that?"

"What the fuck do my clothes have to do with anything?"

"I'd just like to know why you don't dress like everyone else."

Rico expelled another drawn-out sigh. "Honestly?"

"No, Rico. I want you to lie."

"God, you're an asshole."

"Then why don't you make us both happy and partner with someone else?"

"You think I haven't tried? Silva refused my request, so like it or not, I'm stuck with you."

Stuck with him? Dexter hadn't considered that possibility. Just like a thickheaded husband, he'd never considered that Rico's dislike for him was just as strong. He'd only considered his own feelings. If that was an inkling into his married life, no wonder his wife skipped.

"My clothes are camouflage, Dexter, to answer your question. It's something I learned in the military." He talked about the importance of commanding attention, having a sense of what he called "presence."

"I'm a short man," he said, as though Dexter hadn't noticed. "And I work in a world where height is important. So I wear power suits. I'll use any trick in the book to command just an ounce of the respect men like you take for granted."

For once in his life, Dexter was speechless.

"While we're both stuck in this arrangement," Rico continued, "I suggest we make the best of it, and that means I'm included in everything you do, think, or feel while we're on the job. I may not like you and you've certainly made it clear you don't like me, and while I wish it were different, it's not. So let's accept it and figure out how we can work together."

Good God. Was the little shit actually making sense? And was that a smidgeon of respect he was feeling?

"What was the meeting with Madison about?" Rico asked. "I should've been included, not dismissed like an errant child."

He had seemed genuinely glad to meet her, Dexter admitted. So maybe he did have a human side.

"Not everything during the day is job-related, Rico. Like I told you, it was personal."

"Nothing job-related?"

Dexter wasn't sure he could answer that. He thought of Marie, washing her face at a joint in town the night Hawley was shot. If she had been in Yucaipa, why lie about it? Could she have been the woman with Hawley? If so, why would she spend time with a convicted pedophile? To get a story? If that were true, why would she have run from the crime scene, leaving Madison, who was a novice? Questions Dexter knew he'd have to answer. As highly as he thought of her, he was first a cop, and he needed some answers.

Making one of those life decisions, Dexter opened the car door.

"Come on," he said. "We've got work to do."

Inside the squad room, Dexter told Rico about Maddy's conversation.

"I want Searl to see a photo of Marie, but I don't have one and I can't ask her."

"How about the newspaper? Isn't her picture there? You can have it blown up at Kinko's."

"By God, Rico, there might be a brain under that dandy suit after all."

Rico smirked in a satisfied way, but for once, Dexter didn't mind. At last they had a lead.

MADISON KNEW SHE wouldn't be able to face Marie in the morning, so knowing it was the coward's way out, she sent the review by email and enclosed a note saying she'd caught her grandmother's bug. That would give her a couple of days to decide what to do.

She glanced at the clock and realized Gran and Cora would be home soon. She'd fix a light supper for the three of them, and borrowing a phrase from Scarlett O'Hara, she'd worry about Marie tomorrow.

While preparing a pasta salad with shrimp and crusty French bread, she listened for the door. Gran and Cora were late, and Madison was beginning to worry. Where were they? Was her grandmother all right? She hoped the day's outing didn't exhaust her.

When they finally arrived, Cora led Ella to a kitchen chair and shot Madison a silent look.

What did that mean? Had Gran become ill while they were out? Madison would ask as soon as she could get Cora alone.

"Don't fuss," Ella said with a scowl. "I'm all right."

During dinner, Ella only pretended to eat and Madison thought her edginess seemed more apparent than the day before. Her grandmother picked up her knife to butter a slice of bread only to put it back down with a clatter. And once she jabbed her fork into the salad so hard that a stray piece of celery went flying onto the table.

Cora's brows lifted. "You don't have to kill the shrimp, Ella, they're already dead."

"Very funny. You should be on late-night TV."

"If you don't start eating better, you'll be as thin as me," Cora answered. "'Skinny as a rail,' my father always said."

"You do all right."

"Maybe so, but you're built differently. Listen to Madison for once and build yourself up."

Madison listened absently to the two friends' banter, something they'd done for as long as Madison could remember. But now, fork poised close to her mouth, she stared at Cora. Had she really suggested that Ella listen to her? That was a first.

Madison walked Cora down the steps to her car. The evening air felt soft after the day's harsh sun, and the lights in the valley gently spread before them.

"What was that look at dinner about?" She held the door, but instead of sliding behind the wheel, Cora raised her face to the night sky.

"How beautiful the stars are, Madison, and what tiny creatures we are under them. I sometimes wonder at our place in the universe."

Madison waited silently. Whatever it was, Cora was having a difficult time talking about it. That in itself was alarming. She'd never known Cora to be anything but painfully blunt.

"I've known that woman most of my life," Cora finally said, "and we've been best friends for at least thirty of those years. But she's changed. She looks the same, thinner of course, but inside, where it counts, she's different."

Oh, God, Madison thought. Cora had noticed the change in Ella as well. Now she was truly alarmed.

"No matter what life brings," Cora said, "my best friend was always gentle and kind, the yin to my yang. I don't know this woman. She's edgy. Sharp, almost. And she can't make up her mind. One minute she says one thing and the next, another. She's had a personality change."

Cora took Madison by the shoulders. "I hate to even suggest it, but ever since we got back from San Diego, I've been reading up on Alzheimer's, and I think you should ask Ella's doctor about it."

Alzheimer's! Please, God, not that. Please don't let it be that serious.

It wasn't fair, she thought while loading the dishwasher. Not now, not when the work of raising her granddaughter was finally over, not when Madison wanted to spend more time with her doing some fun things together, like traveling to places Ella never had the opportunity to see.

Tomorrow Madison would make an appointment with her grandmother's doctor and take her there, no matter how much she protested.

She prepared two cups of soothing herbal tea and took them to her grandmother in the living room.

"Want some ice cream?"

"I couldn't swallow another bite," Ella told her. "The salad was perfect."

"How could you tell? You didn't eat but two bites."

"Don't give me any sass, Maddy. I'm still strong enough to turn you across my knees."

Madison smiled. "You've never spanked me in your life and you never will."

"And that's your trouble, young lady."

"Drink your tea before it gets cold," Madison said, kissing her grandmother on the cheek.

Ella took a sip, then put the cup on the coffee table.

"I've loved your help, Maddy, but don't you think you should get back to your own life?"

"I will, Gran, just as soon as I feel you're strong enough. Not that there's anything exciting to get back to."

"That's the point. I'm concerned about your life, Maddy. You need to do something, make a life for yourself, not waste it taking care of me."

"A waste? How could anything I do for you be a waste? I love you, Gran, and I consider it a privilege to be with you. But I'm worried about you."

"I'm perfectly fine." Ella picked up the TV remote and scrolled through the channels before putting it down again.

"What is it, Gran? Is something bothering you?"

Ella rested her head on the back of the sofa and closed her eyes. For the long moment before she spoke, Madison studied her pale skin, taking note of the blue veins in her cheeks, the dark circles under her eyes. She was losing weight at an alarming rate. And was that a tear escaping from behind her closed eyes?

What in God's name was wrong?

"I just feel so helpless," Ella whispered, her voice so low Madison had to lean in close to hear, "as if life has spiraled out of control."

"What do you mean, Gran? What's out of control?"

Even though Ella swiped the tear and sat up, her once-proud shoulders curled and her entire body sagged as if the weight she carried was too much to bear.

Madison gently took her grandmother into her arms, holding her in a warm embrace, hoping she could feel the love and support Madison offered.

"What's wrong, Gran? Won't you tell me?"

"We try to do our best, going along in our own little worlds living moral and ethical lives, raising our children to do the same."

"What are you talking about? I don't understand."

"We know evil is out there, but unless or until it touches us, we're not personally involved. And when it does, we're changed. We find ourselves considering things that would have mortified us only a short time before."

"What things, Gran?" Madison took her hand. "You're scaring me."

For the first time, Ella took a long look at her granddaughter, and, during that time, Madison could see the gradual change in her eyes. It was as if she were back from wherever she'd drifted, facing her granddaughter, allaying fears as she'd done since Madison was six. She straightened and her entire demeanor changed.

"Nothing, dear," she said, patting Madison's hand. "I'm

just an old woman who sees shadows when I should be counting my blessings."

"I'm going to make an appointment with your doctor."

"You'll do no such thing. There's nothing wrong with me that a little rest won't cure, and I'm not going to pay that quack good money just to tell me so. Now I don't want to hear another word about it." She rose from the sofa. "I'm going to bed."

Madison knew whatever was bothering her grandmother would remain a mystery until Ella was ready to talk about it, and nothing Madison could say or do would convince her to say anything more.

She'd keep a close watch on her, and if the problem got worse, she'd get her to a doctor no matter what it took.

BRANDON SEARL, WEARING JEAN shorts and flip-flops, led Dexter and Rico into the living room of the mobile home near the shopping center.

Geared toward families, the community court had a swimming pool and basketball hoops at the recreation center. Palm trees dotted the paved streets and couples were walking, enjoying the cooler night air.

Once seated, Mrs. Searl offered lemonade, explaining that it was from the lemon tree in the back yard.

"I don't know what I can tell you that I haven't said before," Searl said.

Dexter handed him an eight-by-ten photograph of Marie.

"I'd appreciate if you'd take a look at this and see if you can identify this woman."

Searl studied the photograph. "She looks familiar, but I can't place her." He passed it to his wife beside him on the overstuffed sofa.

"Could she have been the woman with Hawley?" Dexter asked.

"Possibly. I don't know. I just saw her for a few moments."

"Honey," his wife said. "Isn't she with the newspaper? I think I've seen her photo with her column."

"Of course! That's why she looks familiar."

Dexter took back the photo and handed it to Rico, who retrieved a small box of colored pencils from his coat pocket.

"What did the straw hat look like? What color was it?"

Searl shrugged. "What color's straw? Brown? No, tan. Sorta light tan."

"How big was it?"

Searl frowned, then drew a wide circle in the air around his head.

"I don't know. Big. Covered her head and most of her face. At least the top part."

Rico drew a hat, colored it, and showed it to Searl. "Like this?"

"I suppose. But I still can't say this woman is the one."

"What kind of blouse did she have on?" Dexter asked.

"How am I supposed to remember something like that?"

"Try."

"Now that I think about it, it was…different. Roomy, like a big man's shirt. A bluish-plaid, I think. And it was loose, sorta draped over her clothes."

"Draped over her clothes?" Dexter repeated, exchanging a glance with Rico. That opened all sorts of possibilities.

People usually draped something over their clothes to protect them. What would the woman with Hawley want to protect her clothes from? Blood? If so, that would mean she knew he was going to be shot. Had she been the one to pull the trigger or had she had an accomplice? After all, older women were not usually killers.

So who else had been involved?

"Try a blue-plaid shirt over Marie's blouse," Dexter said. Rico drew the shirt, then handed it back to Searl, only to have him shrug.

A few moments later, Dexter and Rico returned to the Tahoe.

"One good thing came out of tonight, even if Searl couldn't identify Marie." Dexter eased onto Valley Road. "It's looking more and more like the mystery woman was the shooter. Or at least knows who was."

"Now if we can only find her."

SIXTEEN

When Dexter's cell phone rang on the way to work the next morning, he hoped it was Josh. He was surprised to see Marie's name.

"Hey, friend," she said, "I still haven't heard about a special council meeting, so what's up? Do you know when Bates will be sprung?"

"I'll have to get back to you on that. Have to make a couple of calls." Dexter waited for Marie's response, but for once, she went silent. The pause stretched so long that Dexter wondered if the call had been dropped. "Marie? You there?"

"I'm running the story tomorrow," she quickly said, running the words together so it sounded like one long word. Dexter had to say it himself before he got what she was saying.

"What? You can't! Ella's been ill and I haven't had a chance to talk to them."

"I've honored your request to wait up to now, but this is news, Dex, news the community has the right to—"

"Cut the crap, Marie. Are you at the office?"

"Where else?"

"I'm coming by. I need to talk to you."

"Sorry, Dex. I think the world of Madison and Ella, but it's set. I have to release the story. The entire community is affected by—"

"See you in fifteen minutes."

He clicked off and punched Josh's number. Even though

it was before eight, Dexter knew his friend was an early riser. He heard a click, then finally, it rang. And rang.

Come on, Josh! After several rings, the voice mail clicked on. Damn. Where the hell was he, and why hadn't he returned Dexter's calls?

The newspaper parking lot was vacant except for Marie's 4Runner and one other car.

She poured coffee for both of them.

"Got any of the doughnuts you cops are famous for?"

"I didn't take the time," he told her, dropping onto the other office chair. It whooshed in protest. "Listen, Marie. I'm officially asking you to hold the story a couple more days."

"Sorry, Dexter, can't do it. The owner got word about Bates and demanded that I run it."

"Christ-all-Friday! How the hell did that happen? Did you tell him?"

"Of course not. I don't know how he found out, but he did, and he says to run it. I have no choice."

"You must make some excuse and hold the story, at least a couple more days. I'll stop by Ella's today, but they should have more time to adjust before a big fat article in the paper slaps them in the face."

"I've always juggled stories when you've needed confidentiality, Dexter, out of respect for procedure, and because you've asked. But I can't hold this any longer. You'll just have to talk to Madison and Ella today."

Dexter had never abused a woman before and detested men who did, but the urge to shake Marie was so strong that he made for the door to put distance between them.

"I'm not surprised you have no regard for Maddy's reaction, Marie. After all, you didn't think about her the night of the shooting."

"What are you talking about?"

"I'm talking about Jimmy's Steakhouse. I know you were here, in town, instead of on the coast. I have a witness."

She blanched white, but said nothing.

"Just what was so important that you'd place Maddy at a violent crime scene?"

"That was unfortunate, but I don't owe you an explanation."

"Do you have a straw hat, Marie?"

"A straw—oh, my God. You think I was the woman with Hawley that night? You know me, Dex. You know I couldn't do something like that."

"I've begun to wonder if I know you at all. Do you want to tell me about that night here or in the squad room?"

"You wouldn't!"

"This is a murder investigation, and I'll do what's necessary."

"After all the years we've worked together, you have the audacity to ask me something like that? Go to hell. I'm not telling you a damned thing."

Dexter said nothing, but his lips thinned. Keeping eye contact with her, he punched Rico's number on his phone.

"I'm at the newspaper office," Dexter told Rico, "and I want you to question Marie Campbell. I have to leave on an urgent matter, but I'll wait until you arrive."

"You son of a bitch," Marie said after he slipped his phone back into his pocket. "You're actually going to question me about that pervert's murder?"

"Where were you, Marie, and what was so important that you'd risk sending Maddy over the emotional edge?"

"Unless you arrest me," she said, her voice cold, "I don't have to answer any questions. And by the way, aren't you forgetting to read me my rights?"

"You're not in a custodial situation. That means you're free to leave at any time."

"May I remind you that you're in my office? If anyone leaves, it'll be you." When Dexter said nothing, she added, "Why don't you arrest Mayor Goodman? He hasn't said where he was that night. For that matter, pick any female off the streets and ask her. You'll get just as far."

"Right now I'm not interested in the mayor's where-abouts that night. I'm interested in yours. Why were you at a bar in town? And why were you washing your face? Was it to wash off splattered blood? Do you have a blue-plaid man's shirt?"

With a look of disgust, Marie turned her back to him and punched keys on her computer. That suited Dexter just fine. Two could play at that game.

When Rico arrived, Dexter apprised him of the situation.

"Shall I take her in for questioning?" Rico asked.

Marie spun her chair around.

"You've got to be kidding. This has gone far enough, Dexter."

"Just talk to her," Dexter told him, not bothering to lower his voice. "See if she'll tell you anything about that night. I have to leave."

"I'm still running the story tomorrow," Marie said, turning her back to them again.

Now, sitting in his Tahoe, Dexter wanted to hit some-thing. In all of his years on the job, he'd never felt this frus-trated. Always before, there had been something he could do to maintain the illusion he was in control. But now, for the first time in his life, he truly felt helpless. He'd received zilch cooperation from Marie, and as a result, he had to do the one thing he'd prayed he would never have to do—tell Maddy that her nightmare was about to come true.

He'd rather face a Mafioso hit man.

Maybe it was a good thing he'd never had children. He had just seen what concern over Maddy's well-being could do to him, what it could drive him to say. In normal circumstances, he would never have mentioned his suspicions about the straw-hat lady to Marie, but his emotions overrode his judgment.

Emotional detachment was the mantra every law enforcement officer learned, and for good reason. Once an officer becomes emotionally involved, good judgment flies out the window. Mishaps occur, and in their line of work, one mishap could cost lives. His run-in with Marie showed that his judgment had slipped.

Slipped? Hell, it had taken a nosedive.

Maybe it was time to cash it in. That campsite next to a river had never looked so good.

His phone rang. Josh, thank God. He'd been down with a virus, but he estimated the paperwork on Bates would be completed in two weeks or less.

Two weeks! Dexter could kiss his vacation goodbye. No way in hell could he be out of the state when that asshole showed up.

He wished he had two weeks to prepare Maddy and Ella, but time had run out.

If only Felicia could join him today, even for just an hour or two. He decided to call again to make one last plea.

"It's down to the wire, Felicia," he told her. "I have to tell Maddy and Ella now. Today. I know your circumstance, but could you possibly come for a couple of hours, just to stand by in case Maddy needs you? I'll pay for your tickets, pick you up at the airport, and take you back. You'd only be gone a few hours."

"Dexter, I told you. I can't possibly leave right now, and

that's the end of it. I've called my associate and he'll work Madison in tomorrow."

"That's not good enough," Dexter said. "I need help today."

"I'm sorry. That's the best I can do."

"Christ. What do your other patients do in a crisis, Doctor? Slit their wrists?"

"That's not fair."

"Few things in life are."

He clicked off and held his phone, staring at it as if it were his enemy, dreading the call he had to make.

He had never been a man to postpone the inevitable, but now he wished he were anywhere on earth other than right here, right now, forced into an action he'd prayed he would never have to perform.

He punched the speed dial.

"Hey, sweetheart. Is Ella awake? How's she doing? I need to stop by."

MADISON HUNG UP and wiped her hands on the dish towel slung over her shoulder. Something major was wrong. No matter how hard Dexter had tried to act as if nothing were the matter, he'd had *that* sound to his voice, that strained, forced tone he used when he was trying to keep her from hearing something really horrible.

He'd used it when she was growing up and asked about a murder she had heard on the TV or radio. Dexter believed in honesty, so he'd always answered her questions, but she knew he glossed over the details and made a point of sounding as detached as possible.

She stacked the breakfast dishes, carried them to the sink, and wiped the table. She'd let her grandmother know he was coming, and concentrate on staying calm and strong for her.

She heated the cinnamon rolls she'd made to tempt Ella's appetite, then put on a pot of coffee. It was only when she dropped the carafe, spilling water all over the counter and her shoes, that she realized her hands were trembling.

SEVENTEEN

DEXTER TRIED TO relax in the house that was as familiar as his own, but he couldn't get comfortable. He sat on the edge of Ella's overstuffed wing chair, his favorite, but even after stretching out his legs, he still felt too large and awkward.

He moved to the love seat and then back to the wing chair, aware that Ella and Maddy were watching him closely, glancing back and forth at one another, Ella's face growing more pinched by the minute.

"Are we playing musical chairs?" Maddy's voice was pitched higher than normal.

"Whatever it is, Dexter," Ella said with a surprisingly firm voice, slipping one arm around Maddy protectively, "you might as well get it over with."

Dexter nodded, took a swallow of his too-hot coffee, and burned his tongue. He set down the cup.

"Honey, I have some bad news. About Michael Bates."

Madison wrapped her arms around herself. "I don't want to hear this."

Ella held her tighter, and Dexter moved out of his chair to kneel in front of her. He took her cold hands in his.

"Don't be afraid, honey. I'm right here with you. But you have to know what's happening. You have to be prepared. I've done everything I could to avoid this, and so has the senator, but Bates had another parole hearing—"

Madison rocked back and forth, clutching herself, repeating, "I don't want to hear this," over and over.

"Look at me, Maddy. You have to know. This time he was granted parole."

"No, no, no," Madison chanted.

"He'll be released in about two weeks, maybe less. You have to be prepared."

Madison stiffened and stopped rocking. Her eyes went wide.

"Oh, honey," Ella said and tried to hold her granddaughter. "I'm so sorry…"

Dexter gripped her hands harder. "Honey, listen to me. You have to know this. I, and all the other law enforcement officers in the area, will keep him under surveillance at all times. But he will be coming here, to Yucaipa."

"Here?" Madison moaned, then began a low keen, sounding like a wounded animal in too much pain to do anything except cry a mindless sound of agony. Her breathing became rapid and shallow. Her eyes lost focus.

"Maddy!" Dexter said, rubbing her hands, her arms. "Madison, look at me! Can you hear me?"

He checked her pulse. "It's too rapid," he told Ella. "She's going into shock. Call 9-1-1 and bring me a blanket." He briskly rubbed her shoulders, her arms.

Ella made the call and hurried from the room.

When Ella returned with blankets, he wrapped them around Madison. She'd begun rocking again and making that terrible sound.

"Are you all right, Ella?"

"Call her doctor, Dexter," she said, holding Madison tightly. "He'll know what to do." She recited the number from memory.

Cursing the justice system, Bates, Dr. King, the newspaper, and himself for not being able to protect Maddy, Dexter made the call.

Two hours later, he and Ella perched on chairs beside Madison's hospital bed. The ER doctors had knocked her out with sedatives, and Dr. Conners, the jean-clad resident shrink, held a telephone consultation with her family physician and Dr. King's associate. They decided to keep watch for twenty-four hours.

"I must caution you about Madison's state of mind," Conners told them. "When she wakes, she could function as normal, which is what we hope for. Or, she might not."

"What do you mean, 'she might not'?" Ella asked.

"I want you to be prepared, but let's not look for trouble before we see it. We'll evaluate her condition when she wakes."

"Sorry, Doc," Dexter said. "That doesn't cut it. If there's anything we need to know, tell us now."

Conners seized a straight chair from the next bedside, turned it around, and straddled it. His curly black hair stuck out in all directions.

"Judging from my consultation with Dr. Simmons, Madison has lived in a state of angst for many years, and from what you told me when she was admitted, she has just suffered from a severe psychological shock relating to a past traumatic event."

Dexter's lips thinned to a tight line. "I'd just given her some terrible news."

Ella patted his hand. "Don't blame yourself, Dexter. There was nothing else you could do. You had to tell her. You had to tell both of us."

"The human mind is a complicated thing," the doctor went on, "and we still don't know everything about it. When she wakes, she could, as I said, be entirely normal. On the other hand, it's also possible she might suffer from a type of disassociation, even a lapse of memory. While she may recover physically, she may experience a behavior disturbance. As I said, we'll do an evaluation once she awakens."

"When will that be?"

"Oh, she should be coming around in another hour or two," he assured them. "Her own mental health doctor, Dr. Simmons, should be here by then."

"Her own doctor, Dr. King, didn't feel it was necessary to make the trip to see her," Dexter said, his irritation obvious, "so she pawned Maddy off on her associate, who still isn't here. If I were in charge, I'd tell them both to go to hell and ask you to take her case. At least you seem to care."

"That can be arranged," Ella said. "I have power of attorney."

"Hold on a moment," Conners said. "I'm sure Doctors King and Simmons are fine physicians and have legitimate reasons for whatever decisions they've made. Don't be premature here. Let's just wait and see what happens when Madison wakes."

After Conners left, Dexter took Ella's hand and together they watched Maddy sleep. He thought of all the other times through the years he and Ella had taken turns sitting by her bedside after another of her nightmares.

Fat lot of good that did now. What she needed, what she had to have, was protection from Bates. And so far, he hadn't been able to do a damned thing.

"I could use some coffee." Ella rose carefully, as if each movement were an effort.

Alarmed by her evident fatigue, Dexter shot from the chair. He was such a dolt. Because he'd been so concerned about Maddy, he hadn't stopped to realize how Ella must be feeling. She had been such a rock for so many years that he'd taken her strength for granted. He suddenly realized how important she'd been, not just to Maddy all these years, but to him as well.

At the nurse's station, he explained that Ella had been ill and asked for a recliner or easy chair. When the nurse couldn't tell him where one was located, he went on the hunt until he found one tucked into a side corridor. Not wanting to scoot the thing down the hall and disturb others with the noise, he called Rico.

While waiting, he poured coffee in the nurse's station and took Ella a cup. Maddy was still sleeping, so they spoke quietly in the hushed room.

"I had the strangest feeling you knew what I was going to tell Maddy," he told her.

"When you passed up the cinnamon rolls, I knew. Human beings are funny, Dex. I've lived in fear of this very thing for years. Every time I read about a killer being paroled, my heart turned over. I hoped and prayed it would never happen, but I always knew there was the possibility. I just hoped that by the time it did, Maddy would've been stronger."

"Like you?"

"I'm not so strong. It's just that after living nearly seventy years, I've learned that things happen, and you either have to figure out how to adjust or do what's necessary to protect your loved ones. Survival, Dexter, is the key, and I intend on seeing that Maddy survives. No matter what."

Dexter had no reply, so he sipped his coffee in silence.

Rico arrived, and he helped Dexter lug the recliner to Maddy's room. Rico said the usual things one says when visiting someone in the hospital, then went silent, shifting from foot to foot.

Dexter led him to the hallway.

"How'd it go with Marie?"

"She wouldn't answer my questions or even look at me."

When a lab tech hurried past, pushing a cart loaded with small rattling bottles, some obviously filled with blood, Rico went pale.

Dexter took pity and dismissed him. This time Rico offered no argument.

Three hours later, long after the hospital staff had gathered lunch trays, Madison still hadn't awakened. Dr. Simmons hadn't arrived, and Dexter was pacing the floor.

Ella sat on Madison's bed and took her hands. "Maddy, honey, it's Gran. Wake up, now. It's time to wake up."

Madison slept on.

"Something's wrong, Dexter."

Dexter stopped his pacing and studied Madison's face. Alarmed by the stillness, he went to the other side of her bed and sat opposite of Ella.

"Wake up, Maddy." When there was no response, he commanded her again. "This is Dexter, and I'm telling you to wake up! Now!"

Still nothing.

He slapped his hands in a loud crack. Ella flinched, but Madison didn't respond, not even with the flicker of an eyelash.

"Good God!" Dexter jumped from the bed, ran for a nurse, and demanded a doctor. Immediately.

When, after a tense half hour, the doctor still had not appeared, Ella called their family physician, old Doc Hayes.

He arrived in jeans, his white hair in a ponytail, and after exchanging pleasantries with Ella and shaking hands with Dexter, he began his examination.

He read the chart at the foot of Madison's bed, then took a flashlight from his coat pocket and directed the light into her eyes. He ran a ballpoint pen across the soles of her feet. He did as much as he could, then with a sigh, tucked the flashlight away. His expression when he looked up told Dexter the doctor was at a loss.

"I see no medical reason why she hasn't awakened," he said. "The sedatives administered in the ER wore off hours ago, and the preliminary tests show no physical abnormality." He slid onto one of the hard plastic chairs and groaned. "Lord, I wish the hospital could spend some money on decent chairs."

"They're trying to drum up business," Ella said. "After visitors sit in these things a while, they need a doctor."

Dr. Edward Hayes' blue eyes crinkled in delight.

"I'm glad you haven't lost your sense of humor, Ellie. You just may need it."

"What's that supposed to mean?" Dexter asked. "What do you think is wrong?"

"I'm afraid that's beyond my area of expertise. Didn't you say you'd called Dr. Conners? He's young, but he's a bright boy."

"Okay, Teddy," Ella said. "We realize your opinion isn't official, but you've treated Maddy all her life. Surely you must have an idea. Right now, that would be a help."

Dexter knew the story about Ted Hayes and Ella, how they'd dated long before Ella married her husband, and that, since then, he'd been the family doctor, even when Madison's parents had been alive. While he might be past the accepted retirement age, his ideas were young. He still rode his Harley, and when he didn't have the time for long jaunts, he took weekend rides up the mountain to Big Bear.

"What's been going on in her life since I last saw her?" he asked now. "Has anything traumatic occurred?"

"It's been a nightmare," Ella answered, "and it began over a week ago."

Dexter told him about finding Madison at the crime scene at Jimmy's, then about flying to San Quentin for

Bates' hearing, and finally, about telling Maddy and Ella about Bates' release.

Hayes nodded. "Off the record, I'd say she doesn't want to wake up."

"Are you saying Maddy is controlling her sleep?"

"Not consciously," the doctor replied, "but in my years of practice, I've seen this before. I'm no expert, you understand, but it's as if the conscious mind is protecting itself by retreating to a safe place. Shamans believe that when we suffer a trauma, part of our soul flees, a sort of a self-protective mechanism so we can survive the pain. Psychologists call it disassociation."

"So how long will she sleep?"

"I can't say. I doubt anyone can."

"Give me your best guess."

"She could awake at any moment, or she may sleep for a month or more."

"God, no," Ella murmured.

"Isn't there anything we can do?"

"Not that I know of, but Conners would have more knowledge about medical advances in this field."

"What would a shaman do?" Dexter couldn't believe he was asking such a thing, but he was desperate.

"From what I understand, it's quite a ritual, but basically, a shaman would work to retrieve the soul."

Dexter dropped onto a chair. *Retrieve her soul?*

Were he and Ella desperate enough to try a damned fool thing like that?

EIGHTEEN

TWO DAYS LATER, Maddy was still comatose, and Dexter had to fight the urge to shake the doctors into immediate action. He knew they had ordered tests that included an EEG, an MRI, a CT scan, and even a Glasgow Outcome Scale, which adds or subtracts points during an examination of the comatose patient's eye, motor, and verbal or nonverbal responses. But none of the tests helped his frustration when he watched Maddy's pale form sink further into oblivion.

Even though Ella had power of attorney and the final decisions were hers, she always asked Dexter's opinion when the doctors suggested a course of treatment. A catheter had been inserted, and a feeding tube was mentioned. Dexter was horrified.

"You don't think she'll be unconscious long enough for that, do you?"

But it seemed that no one could answer his question. Doc Hayes explained the tube.

"Since she can't take food directly, a tube is simply a device to get nourishment into Madison's system to help her recover. The IV drip ensures she doesn't become dehydrated, but the human body needs more. If she doesn't regain consciousness by tomorrow, they'll begin treatment."

"What will that involve?" Ella asked.

"They'll try the NG tube first, as sort of a temporary measure. It's much smaller in diameter than the permanent tube." He explained the procedure. "When she recovers, the NG can easily be pulled out. It's a simple process, actually."

"You mentioned a smaller tube as a temporary measure, Teddy," Ella said, her voice as frail as she looked. "What's the difference?"

"The permanent tube requires surgery," Hayes told them, "but I don't think she'll need that. In any case, you can discuss that option with a surgeon if it becomes necessary. Let's just hope it won't be."

After Hayes left, Dexter took Maddy's hand and willed her to wake. He was alarmed not only by her continued unconsciousness, but also by Ella's failing health. How much of this stress could she take without becoming ill again?

She hadn't left Maddy's bedside and had barely eaten. He'd tried everything, including bribery, to get her to go home and rest, but she'd refused.

"I must be here when Maddy opens her eyes," she told him. "But you need some time away, Dex. Your vacation is coming up soon, isn't it? How long will you be gone?"

His vacation. Green trees, rivers, a paradise that now seemed a distant dream. One day he'd get there, but not now. Not when Maddy needed him.

"I can't leave while Maddy's so ill. I'll be right here as long as the two of you need me."

"But, Dexter, you need a break."

"I'm not leaving," he said with a finality Ella must have recognized. She nodded, patted his hand, and said nothing more.

The article about Bates' parole splashed across the front page of the *Tribune*, although Dexter only read the headline. He knew he was being unreasonable. As a cop, he needed to be abreast of the news, but when it involved

Maddy and Ella, the news became too personal. It still appalled him to think Marie had put her profession first, and he wondered if she had any idea what her actions had caused.

Cora, at times accompanied by Clara, spent almost as much time in the room as Ella, but while Dexter knew the sisters were fond of Maddy, he felt Cora's main concern was for her best friend.

"Ella, you haven't been eating," she said in her usual brisk tone. "Not that I blame you. Hospital food is unfit for healthy people, much less sick ones."

She hoisted a huge cloth tote bag from the floor and dropped it on a chair, and like an Army sergeant on a mission, she marched to the next bed, hijacked the tray, and rolled it to Ella's chair.

Dexter watched with amusement, thanking his lucky stars he'd never been on her wrong side. As big as he was, he was sure that if she considered it necessary, she'd box his ears in an instant.

"I've brought your favorites," Cora told Ella. "Fresh seafood salad with crab, shrimp, and rice, and fruit salad with cream cheese and walnuts."

She took a package of sanitizing wipes from her tote bag and swabbed the top of the tray.

Dexter took a helping and happily crunched on the fresh fruit and walnuts—until he noticed that Ella hadn't touched a bite. He set down his plate.

"Ella, this has gone on long enough. If you don't eat, you'll be flat on your back as well. Do you want to be in the next bed when Maddy wakes? How do you think that'll make her feel? Hasn't she lived with enough guilt?"

At Ella's wounded look, his heart turned over, but his

years of training in the sheriff's department kicked in. Instead of caving, he stared her down.

"Dexter, you don't have to talk to her like that," Cora protested.

"Cora, I'll thank you to butt out." He ignored her quick intake of breath. He might have felt like the serial monster who'd murdered old ladies back in the sixties, but he held Ella's gaze until she sighed and reached for a plate. Only when she took a small bite of her seafood salad did he relax.

"Now chew it up, swallow, and take another bite. Repeat as necessary." He took another forkful of his fruit salad, but for some reason, it no longer tasted as sweet.

Cora scowled at him. "Really, Lieutenant," she snapped. "That wasn't necessary."

"Dexter's right, Cora," Ella said, calmly finishing her salad. "For once, butt out."

"Well!" Turning a bright pink, Cora sat up even more stiffly in her chair.

A timid knock sounded on the door, and Marie appeared, holding a bouquet of summer flowers.

"I'm so sorry," she said first to Ella, then to Dexter. "I'm sorry."

Was that a hint of moisture in her eyes? Never, in all the years he'd known her, had he ever seen her cry.

Ella took the flowers. "It wasn't your fault, Marie. I suppose it was inevitable."

"I'll take care of those flowers," Cora said briskly and left the room. When she returned with a vase, she filled it with water and the flowers, then set it on the bedside stand. "They look nice, don't they? The yellow daisies and pink roses brighten up the room."

"I can't stay long," Marie told them. "I have work to do, but I wanted to check on Madison."

"Are we intruding?" Mr. Chauncey, his white shirt and blue vest as spotless as ever, stood in the doorway. Senator Stone, in a charcoal sports coat, held on to his arm.

"Hello, Dexter," the senator said and nodded to Cora and Marie. "Ella, may we come in?"

Dexter noted the astonishment on Marie's face. He was sure she knew Ella and Maddy were friends with the senator. As a newspaper editor, she had attended a few of his dinner parties with the two women, but from the look on her face, she obviously was surprised to see him take enough of a personal interest to visit Maddy in the hospital.

With the aid of a polished wooden cane, the senator made his way to Ella and took her hand.

"I'm so sorry to hear about Madison, Ella. With the medical advances today, I'm sure it won't be long until she's back on her feet. If there's anything I can do to help, I'm at your service."

"As you always are, Senator. Thank you, I appreciate it. Please have a seat."

"Ah, yes, a seat." He took the chair Dexter had vacated. "This past year I've established a new relationship with chairs. Perhaps we can find one for Mr. Chauncey as well."

"Thank you, but that won't be necessary." Mr. Chauncey assumed a sentry position at the senator's right side.

"I appreciate your concern, Senator, and it was kind of you to make the trip," Ella said, "but how did you discover Maddy was in the hospital?"

"Oh, I have my sources," he replied mysteriously. After a few moments of silence, he smiled. "I'd love to keep all of you thinking I had special powers, but I read the article about Michael Bates in the newspaper. I was concerned. Mr. Chauncey called the newspaper, and someone on your staff, Miss Cox, I believe, told him about Madison."

Everyone's gaze went to Marie.

"I had to do it," she said, her stricken gaze moving from the senator to Dexter, then finally to rest on Ella. "The newspaper has a duty, I have a duty…" Then, with a muffled, "Excuse me," she hurried from the room.

Dexter felt a momentary pang of compassion for her, but his resentment won. He let her go.

Ella gazed at the doorway. "Oh, dear, I do hope she'll be all right. I'll give her a call later."

"It's just like you to worry about everyone else," the senator said. "I'm sure, as a newspaper editor, she's faced tough choices before and has learned to adjust to the consequences. Now tell me about Madison."

It was almost midnight before Dexter left the bull pen and stopped by the hospital. The captain had thrown a couple of new cases at him and demanded that he and Rico spend their time and energy on them instead of chasing shadows.

Dexter knew he should arrange a lineup so Brandon Searl could observe Marie wearing a straw hat, but thinking of the endless hours she'd devoted to various functions for those in need, especially children, he'd delayed putting her through the humiliation. But the feeling that she was involved in Hawley's murder continued to nag at him. Otherwise, how could someone else, especially someone covered with blood splatters, vanish without a trace?

Hell, in his book, anyone who'd killed Hawley should be canonized for eliminating another dirtbag from society. At least with him gone, the children in his town would be safer. Still, as an officer sworn to uphold the law, he couldn't let personal feelings interfere with his duty, couldn't allow citizens, even Marie, to become vigilantes.

The hospital corridor was dimmed, a relief to his tired eyes, and hushed with only the occasional sound of a nurse's shoe squeaking on the tiled floor. From a few doors beyond Maddy's, low-volumed canned laughter erupted from someone's TV.

His steps slowed. What would he find in Maddy's room? Would there be signs of her recovery? He hoped so. He wasn't a praying man, but he prayed now. He wasn't sure he could take several more hours of watching her waste away in a coma.

Greg was sitting by her bed, holding her lifeless hand and whispering to her. His sandy hair was tousled, as if he'd run his hands through it several times.

Dexter stood quietly by the door and waited, then coughed discreetly and entered the room.

Still clutching Maddy's hand, Greg stood.

"Dexter," he said. "I came as soon as I heard." He extended his hand and Dexter took it.

In the corner, Ella was napping in the recliner, a light-weight throw tucked around her. Cora's work, Dexter thought. Instead of the harsh glare over Maddy's bed, a night-light softened her features and threw the tubes and monitor into shadows.

"Hi, sweetheart," Dexter whispered to Maddy's sleeping form. Still no improvement in her condition. He had hoped she'd be awake, although if that had happened, Ella would have let him know.

Greg shrugged, a bewildered, helpless gesture Dexter recognized. "I can't believe this is happening."

"It's hard for all of us to take." Dexter took the other chair, an orange plastic thing so small it could've been made for an elf.

"I'm glad to see you," he told Greg, trying to keep his voice down so Ella could sleep. "Maddy could use a friend."

"I want to be more than a friend, but she won't let me.

I asked her to marry me, and the next thing I knew, she broke up with me."

"I didn't know your relationship had gone that far."

"Obviously it hasn't, and that's the problem."

"Don't give up on her," Dexter urged. "She needs to start living, have a family, and after she recovers from this, I'm going to make a concentrated effort to see that she does."

"Yeah, well, I'd appreciate any help you can give, but I doubt it'll do any good. I don't know if you're aware, but under that soft exterior lies the heart of a very stubborn woman. I doubt anyone can make her do anything she doesn't want to do."

Dexter grinned. "You forget I've known Maddy since she was six. But hey, you're a smart man and a decent-looking one. You started a business in this rough economy and made it a success. Surely you can get one young woman to fall for you."

"I've tried everything, and so far, nothing's worked. When she wakes up, I'll certainly give it another try." He paused, watching Maddy breathe. Then, "She will wake up, won't she?"

"She will if I have anything to say about it."

After Greg left, Dexter took the chair next to the bed. You will wake up, he told Maddy silently, watching her eyelids twitch or a finger move. When it had first happened, Ella and he thought Maddy was waking and excitedly called a nurse, but she said it was just muscle contractions.

Now he looked at the delicate arch of her brows, the blue-veined lids over her blue eyes closed in sleep, with a sense of hopelessness. It wasn't fair. She was a beautiful, sensitive young woman, and if she didn't wake soon, her life would be over before it even began.

Ella made a sound like a long sigh and shifted in the recliner. Even asleep, her face had not lost its haggard look. How much longer could she go on before she collapsed? If she had been awake, he'd give her a hug to comfort her, to share some of his strength with her.

He sat back in the chair and leaned his head against the wall. His bones screamed with fatigue. His skin ached. For one tiny nanosecond, he longed for someone to comfort him.

Here he was, the big, strong, macho man who took care of everyone else, yet he longed for someone to comfort him. How wonderful it would be to feel a woman's soothing arms around him. Perhaps even a wife's.

But he didn't have that and it was his own fault. Sure, he'd been a good provider, always paying the bills, making sure his wife and the few women in his life could buy the things they'd wanted. But he'd never let them have *him*, not in the way they'd needed. He'd always kept his feelings locked tightly out of reach.

It had been the same with Pam. He'd known she'd loved him, but he'd blown it with her as well. Now their relationship was a friendly one, although at times he wished it were more.

The only problem was, he didn't know if he could devote the time to someone else. As he'd grown older, he'd also fallen into a comfortable rut, and now he didn't know if he could ever again have the patience to share his life with someone else.

What a waste. But he could still give it a try if he wanted. Maybe when Maddy recovered and the world was right again, he'd take a late vacation and ask Pam to go with him to West Virginia—just as a friend, of course....

He jerked awake to find it was three-thirty in the morning. Maddy still lay oblivious to everything. Only a few hours until they inserted the feeding tube. A feeding tube, for Christ's sake.

"Damn it, Maddy, wake up!"

He didn't realize he'd spoken aloud until Ella opened her eyes, saw him, and went back to sleep.

Perhaps somewhere in Maddy's subconscious, she could hear him too. What was it Doc Hayes had said about shamans believing that a comatose patient's soul was trying to escape? He'd also said it could be reached. Hell, he wasn't particularly spiritual, but he'd try anything to get Maddy to wake.

He leaned forward and took her hand.

"Wake up, Maddy," he whispered urgently. "You've been sleeping, but now it's time to wake up."

He watched her face for any signs that she had heard him, but she remained just as she had been. He gripped her hands and tried again.

Over the next several hours, he alternated between cajoling her to awake and demanding that she do so. The blackness at the window faded to gray and then finally gave way to the morning light. He could hear voices and the sound of metal rattling. The hospital was coming to life before the shift-change at seven.

Just as Dexter reluctantly stood to leave for work, he thought of the guilt he'd laid on Ella about not eating. Although it had been difficult for him to do, the outcome was that she'd forced herself to eat enough to regain her strength.

Would guilt work with Maddy as well?

Hell, he was desperate enough to try anything.

He sat on her bed and leaned close to whisper in her ear.

"Maddy, you must wake up now. I know you don't want to face what's happening here, but you must think about Ella. Your grandmother hasn't left your side and she's close to collapse. If you want to sleep until you die, I can't stop you, but do you want to take her with you? Is that the way to repay all she's done for you?"

He leaned back and watched her face. Were her eyes moving beneath those nearly transparent lids? Was there a slight change in her breathing?

"Squeeze my hand if you can hear me." He watched for any sign of a response, but there was nothing. If ever in his adult life he'd felt like crying, it was now.

NINETEEN

"So why haven't we pulled Marie Campbell in for a lineup?" Rico asked, slapping paper down on his desk. The morning's *boorah* briefing had faded into the bull pen's normal madhouse of ringing phones, clicking keyboards, and good-natured ribbing between detectives.

"If you don't want to be the bad guy," Rico pushed on, "I'll do it. I don't have a history with her."

"Can it, Rico." Dexter took a long slug of his cold coffee, his eyes scratchy from lack of sleep. He'd barely managed to stay awake through Silva's briefing. He longed to head east on the freeway and drive until he escaped ringing phones, computers, feeding tubes, and hopelessness.

"Dexter!" Silva shouted from his office door. "You and Rico get in here now!"

Christ. What now?

"Uh-oh." Chris was handing Tish a file from across her desk. "Sounds like your vacation's in danger, Dex. What have you done now?"

"Vacation's dead and buried," he told her, shuffling to the captain's office with Rico two steps behind him.

"Hey," Tish piped up, "I got the perfect thing for dead and buried. Viagra. Been on the stuff a month and Mighty Joe is alive again."

"Mighty Joe? Holy hell, now I've heard everything," Bob Frazer, fortyish and fresh from his vacation, laughed. "Shouldn't that be Tiny Tim?"

"You don't believe me, ask my wife." Tish grinned.

"She's walking spraddle-legged." He rubbed his bald head. "I might even grow me some hair again."

Chris shook her head.

In the captain's office, Dexter slumped in the nearest chair.

"You look like shit, Dexter," Silva said, raking the detective with a critical gaze. "I know you've had some personal issues lately, but you're still on payroll. First-year rookies perform better than you've been doing. I've never seen you like this."

He flipped through pages of scrawled notes and blank time sheets.

"Downtown's demanding some action on our backlogs," he went on, "and accounting is on my back. Take my advice, Dexter. Straighten yourself up. Shave. Change your clothes."

"Yes, Captain."

"You better get yourself together damn fast. Downtown's heard enough of my excuses. And you, Rico, you shouldn't be tied to a sinking ship. You still want that transfer?"

Rico shot a look at Dexter.

Now he'd finally get rid of the little prig, Dexter thought. Funny. He thought he'd be happier to have that happen.

"Well?" Silva demanded. "I don't have all day."

"No, sir," Rico said. "I'll stay with Dexter."

An hour later, pulling out of yet another drive-thru for coffee, Dexter popped three antacid tablets and washed them down with coffee.

"You need to eat something," Rico told him, a worried look on his face.

"I'd puke it up."

Rico sipped his hot tea and stared out the window. "I

hope Madison recovers soon or we'll have to bury both of you."

Dexter slammed on the brakes. "Goddammit, Rico! Don't ever say the word 'buried' in the same sentence with Maddy again. Do you hear?"

"Sorry."

Dexter put the car into neutral, got out, and walked around to Rico's side.

"You drive. I'm a disaster waiting to happen."

Rico took the wheel. "You want to stop by the hospital?"

"Hell, no. She'll have that thing stuck in her face and I don't want to see it. It would be like admitting it's all over."

"Where to?"

Dexter leaned his head back and closed his eyes. "You decide. Today, you're lead detective."

Just as they headed out of the parking lot, Dexter's phone rang. For the first time in his career, he didn't answer, didn't even check to see who was calling. He didn't want to hear that the hospital had successfully inserted the feeding tube; he felt too damn tired to do anything except go off by himself and die like an old elephant.

When he didn't answer, Rico's phone rang. He listened briefly, then clicked off.

"Silva said to remind you of the city council meeting today in Yucaipa," Rico told Dexter.

"Like hell."

"He said you'd object. 'It's Dexter's ball game,' he said. 'You tell him to be there.'"

EVEN THOUGH IT was a weekday morning, the council chamber in Yucaipa's city hall overflowed with residents, all demanding answers about Michael Bates' parole.

Mayor Goodman tried to keep order by calling one citizen at a time to the microphone, but despite his admonishment, people interrupted each other by shouting questions. Dexter was astonished. He had never seen the stately city hall so chaotic that the mayor would actually have to continually bang his gavel. Marie was snapping shots of the proceedings. Dexter found the level of tension so unbearable that he told Rico he was getting out of there.

"You can't leave me here alone," Rico hissed. "I'm not familiar enough with Bates' history."

"Improvise."

Just then, the mayor placed his microphone directly in front of the gavel and struck it repeatedly, creating thunderous bangs through the chamber. Dexter's heart slammed into his ribs. God, he had to escape this madhouse.

"Ladies and gentlemen," the mayor said as the room grew quiet, "please remember where you are. If I don't have order, I'll call the meeting to a close and no one, *no one*," he emphasized, "will get answers. Is that what you want?"

For the first time since the proceedings had begun, there was silence, broken only by the scraping sounds made by Dexter's chair as he rose to leave the room. He had nearly reached the door when he heard his name.

"Detective Quinn," the mayor announced. "You were involved in the initial investigation that led to Bates' arrest and incarceration, and you attended parole hearings with Senator Logan Stone. Why don't you step up to the mike and answer a few questions for us?"

Oh, hell. He was trapped. Running his hands through his hair, Dexter made his way to the podium.

"Detective Quinn, please help us to understand why this has happened," a man in the audience called out. "How can a convicted killer be allowed to leave a prison and live among law-abiding citizens?"

"It's not right!" another man about thirty shouted.

"Criminals should rot in prison!" another said. "'Do the crime, do the time.'"

The mayor banged his gavel several more times. "Gentlemen, gentlemen, please. We must keep order."

"I'd like to ask a question." A woman in her forties stood. Her blond hair was swept up and secured by one of those leather clips with a wood stick. She supported an infant on her chest in one of those strap-held carriers.

"I'm Ginny Murken. I take care of my baby granddaughter and I'm concerned about what'll happen in our community once this man is released. I won't feel good about letting my granddaughter play in my yard, or when she gets older, walk to school by herself. This used to be a safe, family community, but first we had Jeff Hawley, and now Michael Bates. How can we protect ourselves when we're surrounded by felons? How can we protect our children?"

When she took her seat, the audience broke out in applause.

Mayor Goodman banged his gavel. "Excellent questions, Mrs. Murken. Perhaps Detective Quinn can offer some explanations."

Dexter swore silently. How the hell could he offer explanations to ease their fears when he had the same concerns?

"I understand your apprehensions, Mrs. Murken, and those of everyone in the community. Frankly, I feel the same. However, according to the law, Mr. Bates has served his time and, as you know, will be released into society."

Shouts of protest rang from the audience. He even heard a "Boo," as if he were emceeing a wrestling match.

"No one wants parolees in their community," he continued, "but the fact is, you already have several. Most towns do, because short of herding them together and putting them on an uncharted island, there's not much else to do with them. The point is rehabilitation, to help them become part of society again."

"Why should my family and I be jeopardized so that felons can live next door to me?" Dexter didn't see the woman who'd asked that question.

"Good point," he responded, "but do you have any other suggestions? As of now, our parole system, with all its flaws, is the best we've got. We have over a thousand state prisons in America, thirty-three just in California with over a hundred-seventy-thousand inmates. We simply do not have the facilities or the money required to house and feed every convicted prisoner for an indefinite length of time.

"And consider the costs involved. Do you know one report, over five years old, stated that correctional authorities spent almost forty billion to maintain the nation's state correctional system in that fiscal year? That's forty billion per year, folks."

"I say save us all some money and issue some old-time justice," someone called out. "Take 'em out and shoot 'em!"

"Aside from the controversial moral issues, executions cost taxpayers even more," Dexter replied, ignoring the jibe. "As long as people break the law, we'll have this problem."

"What can we expect once Michael Bates is released?" a woman asked.

"The county officials will be notified of the exact date of his release, and we'll keep an eye on him. In all probability, he'll be sent to the halfway house and be fitted with a GPS tracking system. If, at any time, he crosses his preset boundaries, law enforcement will be notified instantly. The tracking system is already mandatory for sex offenders, and we hope it'll also be required for other parolees as well."

When his cell phone vibrated, Dexter ignored it at first, and then, thinking it might be news about Maddy, flipped it open and read two simple words.

She's awake.

"Honey? You all right?" he whispered, punching the call button for a nurse.

"I'm okay," she murmured without opening her eyes. "Just…tired, that's all." Without another sound, she drifted off to sleep.

"She's sleeping naturally," the nurse reassured Ella and Dexter after taking Maddy's vital signs. "The doctors will be in shortly, but I think she'll be all right now."

A text message from Marie was waiting when Dexter checked his phone twenty minutes later. Did his leaving the meeting have anything to do with Madison? If so, was there any news of her condition?

He had a few things to say to her, so he stopped by the newspaper office.

She was on the phone, her back to the door and speaking quietly, almost whispering. Yet, the intensity in her voice brought Dexter to a halt.

"That's exactly what I'm saying," she hissed. "She wanted to check my newswire service—" She paused as if to listen, then, "This is mind-boggling, but if it's true, if you're behind such a thing, you'd better end it right now. I haven't forgotten your words years ago—" Dexter must have made a slight noise because she whirred around and blanched white when she saw him.

"Dexter! What are you doing here?" Without another word, she snapped her cell phone shut.

"That sounded ominous."

"Yeah, well, you know how the newspaper business is now. How's Madison?"

Dexter brought her up to speed.

"I'm so sorry, Dexter. I had no idea Madison would ve such a violent reaction."

"That's the problem with all you newspeople," he said, able to control the anger he'd held in check for so long.

TWENTY

DEXTER HUSTLED DOWN the tiled corridors with Rico at a run behind him. Not until he burst into Maddy's room and saw her up and sipping some liquid through a straw did he allow himself to breathe again.

Ella sat on Maddy's bed, helping her to eat from the breakfast tray.

"Try some of your oatmeal," Dexter heard her say. "It'll give you some strength. And for heaven's sake, have some orange juice instead of that soda. It's better for you."

"Your grandmother's right, you know," Dexter said with a big smile. "Soda will rot your insides."

"Dex," Maddy said and held out her arms for a hug.

He leaned down and wrapped his arms around her. "I'm so damned glad to see those blue eyes again. God, let me look at you."

"I...kept dreaming about you," Maddy said, her voi strained and weak, "a strange dream. You grabbed hand and wouldn't let go."

Dexter felt as though his heart would explode with itude.

"So what do the doctors say?"

"Doc Hayes..." Maddy's voice, already a whisp solved as if she simply ran out of energy. When back and closed her eyes, Ella flashed a panicke Dexter. Was she lapsing back into a coma?

Dexter took the cola, set it on the tray, and searched Maddy's face.

"You just want a headline, and you don't even consider how the story affects the people involved. Did you know, after all these years, Maddy still sleeps with all her lights on?"

"Dex—"

"Did you honestly think she'd read that article and say, 'That's too bad,' as if she were reading about an inconvenient traffic jam on I-10? You people are disgusting."

Marie gazed at him with a hurt expression as if she'd been betrayed by her best friend. Then her lips thinned.

"You think cops are less intrusive? Get real, Dexter. Don't you think your personal involvement is clouding your judgment?"

"My personal involvement has kept you out of a lineup so far."

"Come on, Dex. Do you really think I'm capable of murder?"

"Anyone's capable under the right circumstances."

"Do you think I knew Hawley? That I hated him enough to kill him?"

"How the hell do I know? You won't tell me anything about that night."

"You just have to trust me."

"I used to, but you blew it. Now you're on your own."

WHEN MADISON WOKE that afternoon, sunlight was pouring through the window, so she knew it was afternoon. Ella's chair was empty, the other bed stripped. She was alone.

Alone. What would she do if Michael Bates walked into the room? Was he, this minute, on his way to Yucaipa to find her?

Her frantic gaze flew to the IV and to the tube leading to the catheter. Lying there, attached to so many tubes, she felt helpless, vulnerable to anything he wanted to do.

But surely, she tried to rationalize, if he were anywhere near her, if there was any way he could get to her, Dexter wouldn't have left her alone.

No one had mentioned him when she'd awakened earlier, and she'd been too groggy to ask. Was he out of San Quentin now?

When the bathroom door opened and her grandmother appeared, Madison was so relieved to see her she could have cried.

"You're awake." Ella sat beside her on the bed. She finger-brushed her granddaughter's hair back from her forehead, just as she'd done when Madison was little and woke terrified from a nightmare. "How do you feel?"

"Gran, what about Michael Bates? Is he out yet?"

Ella sighed and reached for Maddy's orange juice. "Take a sip. You need nourishment."

Madison drank. "Gran, tell me about Bates."

"He's still in prison, and Dexter doesn't know the exact date of his release yet. But the important thing is to get you well."

When Ella moved to the recliner, Madison noticed the slump in her grandmother's stance, the wrinkled navy pullover and the dirty smudges dotting her white pants. Hadn't she been home to change clothes or to have a decent night's sleep? Her face was gray, her hair matted. Madison couldn't remember a time when her grandmother hadn't cared about her appearance.

"Gran, go home. You need rest."

"I'll go home when you do."

Madison heard the firm conviction and knew changing her grandmother's mind was as likely as the Mojave Desert sprouting tea roses, so she did the next best thing.

She vowed to gain strength as quickly as possible so they could both go home.

If her fears were ever to come true, she knew she'd need all the strength she could get.

TWENTY-ONE

JERICHO WELCOMED EACH new arrival with the usual handshake. This time, their meeting featured a buffet lunch with freshly peeled kiwi, croissants, and bowls of strawberries and cream.

"How are you, Number Three?" Jericho inquired, buttering a croissant. "With all the taxes on tobacco, I'm sure you're glad you gave it up years ago."

Number Three wore his usual jeans, but today his smoking jacket was a brilliant red. He patted the pipe in his pocket.

"I am glad, but for different reasons. The day I let some do-gooder dictate what I can or cannot enjoy in my life is the day I'm ready for an old-folks home."

"Hear, hear." They all clicked their water glasses with a spoon to register their agreement.

When they'd finished their meals, Jericho picked up a file. As before, all conversation stopped.

"The scheduled date for Michael Bates' execution is approaching," Jericho told them after the servant had cleared the table and left the room, "and all systems are in place. I believe we can proceed to new business: Latisha Woodward, twenty-three years old, Bossier City, Louisiana."

Number Three gasped. *"A woman?"*

"I know it's unusual," Jericho said, setting down the file, "but times have changed."

"I'm certainly grateful for that," Number Four said, straightening her suit jacket.

"Does anyone have a serious problem with executing a woman?" Jericho asked. "If so, let me remind you that women can commit as heinous crimes as men, and as perpetrators, they must be brought to justice—in one way or another, regardless of their sex. If we can't agree on that point, there's no need to go further. I think it's time for a straw poll. Number Two?"

All eyes fixed on the bearded gentleman with the troubled eyes. He smoothed his white mustache and beard before answering.

"While I'm aware that women commit ghastly crimes," he began, "I'm also from the old school. I believe our women are the gentle sex, even the better one, and I treat them as such."

"Yes, you do," Number Four interjected. "Your courtesies remind me of my schoolgirl days and I enjoy them. But women today are heads of corporations and heads of state. We make life and death decisions, as evidenced by this organization."

"Please don't take offense, Number Four. Just because I believe women are the gentle sex doesn't diminish my appreciation of their ambitions and capabilities. That should be obvious." His eyes met Jericho's.

Number Five spoke up. "But what if a woman, such as Ms. Woodward, commits a heinous crime? Shouldn't she be punished as if she were a man?"

"I suppose so," Number Two replied. "After all, that's why we're here. I simply find the idea abhorrent."

"But can you overcome your reservations to do what's necessary?" Jericho asked.

"What has the Woodward woman done? If it's monstrous enough, perhaps I'll overcome my reluctance."

"Very well." Jericho picked up the file. "According to the police records, neighbors called 9-1-1 after hearing screams from her apartment. When deputies arrived, they found the body of a four-year-old boy, her son, unconscious, lying in a pool of his own urine. His body was covered with bruises, and he still had the imprint of a hand on his left cheek. A tiny cut was visible under his left eye. In spite of the emergency medical treatment, the child died two hours later. The coroner's report indicated a massive abdominal hematoma and numerous broken ribs. The mother claimed her son, Tommy, had fallen down the apartment stairs, but the coroner believed the child had been kicked to death."

Jericho set down the file. "Is that monstrous enough, Number Two?"

"I'm appalled."

Murmurs of agreement sounded in the room.

"Fine, then," Jericho said, consulting the file again. "It seems that the mother had never been married and had no visible means of support. She had been incarcerated numerous times for solicitation, and officers found drug paraphernalia in the home.

"At trial, first-degree murder charges were dropped when the prosecution could not prove, despite several scars, that the child had been abused. A new trial on child neglect resulted in Ms. Woodward's eight-month incarceration. However, she's now back in her apartment, watching her neighbor's three-year-old toddler, who, unfortunately, just happened to fall down the same stairs as her son. The child survived, but is currently hospitalized with several fractured ribs. Ms. Woodward is expecting her second child, and she's due to deliver any day." Jericho paused long enough to meet each member's eyes, then proceeded.

"We all agree, do we not, that if an infant is orphaned, that child would have an excellent chance of being adopted by caring parents?"

After the members agreed, the vote was taken, the decision announced, and the members retired to the leather chairs for a bit of socializing before leaving. Jericho, along with Number Two, pulled Number Six to the side.

"I have a bit of other business I'd like you to execute."

"I'M READY TO hear about Michael Bates now," Maddy told Dexter. Snugly wrapped in a soft afghan Ella had knitted years ago, she sat on her grandmother's porch overlooking the sparkling lights of the city below. Ella rested in the patio chair beside her, her feet propped up on the ottoman that Dexter had hauled from the living room. He sat on the lounge chair between them, his long legs stretched in front of him, happy that Maddy was finally out of the hospital. In the kitchen, Cora and Clara were helping Greg with dinner.

"I'm sorry I reacted so horribly when you tried to tell me before," Maddy continued, "but if you'll give me another chance, I'm ready. I need to know."

"You just got out of the hospital today." Dexter hedged, reluctant to talk about anything that might spoil her recovery. "Let's just enjoy the fresh air, the company, and the good food."

The screen door opened. "Am I interrupting something?" Greg wiped his hands on the towel slung over his shoulder.

"Nothing that can't be discussed later," Dexter replied, glad for a reprieve.

"But, Dexter," Maddy started to protest.

"Let's have a nice dinner and celebrate your homecoming. Then we'll talk about it. Tomorrow might be good. Okay, Maddy?"

She nodded, but Dexter could tell from her expression she wasn't happy.

"I can delay dinner a few minutes," Greg suggested, looking from Dexter to Madison, no doubt sensing the tension. He had stopped by with a pot of fresh stew and had taken over Ella's kitchen to prepare a salad and bake the corn muffins he'd premixed.

"Of all the nerve," Maddy had said when Greg carted his pots and pans into the kitchen. Ella had been delighted and had ignored Maddy's scowls. Cora and Clara followed to help him prepare dinner.

But even though Maddy frowned and grumbled, barely answering whenever Greg spoke to her, Dexter noted that she watched him intently whenever he came into view.

"We're fine," Dexter told Greg. "Now, how about dinner out here?" He threw his legs over the side of his chair and carefully rose from the low chaise. "Now that the sun's down, there's a nice breeze, and after a week at the hospital, the outside air feels wonderful."

"I'll set the patio table," Ella said and went inside.

Twenty minutes later, Maddy sat back from the table, most of her stew still in the bowl.

"What's the matter?" Greg asked with a frown. "Didn't you like it?"

"It was delicious, but I couldn't hold more than a couple of bites. I'll save the rest for lunch tomorrow."

"Good idea," Ella said, finishing her small helping. She buttered her second muffin. "You must give me the recipe, Greg."

Dexter ladled another helping of the stew. "Sure beats a burger joint or frozen dinners."

"Now wait a minute." Greg set down his spoon. "Not that I'm fishing for compliments, but that's not saying much. Can't I get some raves here?"

"Sounds like fishing to me." Maddy gently dabbed her

mouth with the napkin, as if she were seated at a formal English tea, then set the cloth next to her plate.

Ella nearly rolled her eyes. "I think dinner was fantastic, and I don't mind buttering up the cook. Thank you, Greg." She leaned over to give him a kiss on the cheek. "I hope you'll do it again sometime. Anytime."

Maddy threw a scorched look at her grandmother, and Ella simply shrugged. Dexter watched with amusement and took a sip of coffee to hide a grin. If he knew Maddy at all, he'd swear, no matter how she might protest, that she was smitten.

"It was delicious, Greg," Clara said. "And the muffins were the best I've ever had."

Cora glared at her sister. "They were tasty, I admit, but the best? I always thought you liked mine."

"I do. It's just that Greg's were sweeter, more like cake."

Cora sniffed. "If I'd wanted cake with dinner, I'd have baked one. True corn bread is never sweet. It's crusty. All you young people think you have to pour sugar into everything. What's happened to good, old-fashioned cooking?"

Forks froze in midair. All eyes went to Greg, whose face had that deer-caught-in-the-headlight look. Dexter felt sorry for him.

"Of course you're right, Cora," Greg managed to say. He even smiled. "I bet you make yours the best way, the way my mother and grandmother taught me—the unsweetened batter poured into a hot iron skillet to form a crust and then baked in the oven. There's nothing like that first crunchy bite dripping with fresh butter. But it is nice to occasionally try variations of our favorites, isn't it?"

"I suppose variety can be a good thing—in moderation, of course."

"If you'd be willing to share your recipe," Greg told her, "I'd love for you to supervise a special cooking session at my restaurant. At your convenience, of course. We'll name the corn bread after you, announce it to the customers, and add it to the menu."

For a moment, even Cora seemed speechless. "I think that could be arranged," she finally said before calmly returning to her meal.

Everyone breathed again. Strike a hundred points for Greg, Dexter thought.

Ella fixed her granddaughter with a glare. "It wouldn't hurt you to say something nice. He spent a lot of time that night at the hospital."

Greg's face turned a slow pink. "You were asleep, weren't you?"

"Of course—most of the time."

Dexter enjoyed the silent play between Maddy and Greg and knew he would be a perfect match for her. He was a hardworking, determined young man, and Dexter knew, from the moment he'd overheard Greg talking to Maddy at the hospital, how much he cared. She needed to open her heart, but after what she had already been through, not to mention what was coming up with Bates' release, that would take some effort. He just hoped Greg had a lot of patience.

After dishes were cleared and all six relaxed on the porch, the conversation drifted to the shooting at Jimmy's.

"Have there been any leads on the woman in the straw hat?" Greg asked Dexter.

"Sorry, can't talk about it."

"I've been curious. I haven't seen anything more about it in the *Tribune*."

Dexter shrugged.

"Well, here's something you can discuss," Maddy said. "Tell us about Bates."

"Wouldn't it be better to wait for this discussion after you've had a good night's sleep? Or until we're alone?"

"Everyone here is quite aware of what's happening. Besides, I have to know, and we might as well get it over with. Is he out yet?"

Dexter was cornered. "Okay, honey. If that's what you want, we'll discuss it now." He sat back in his chair.

"My contact says that it might be another week before Bates will actually be released. Like most state agencies, they're short on staff and behind on paperwork. It all takes time to process."

"Only a week," Maddy said softly, "then that monster will be loose. I thought it would be longer. But go on. I want to know everything."

Dexter wondered if the determination to talk about Bates signaled a change in her attitude, a willingness to finally face her past. He repeated the information about Bates going to a halfway house. "That'll give everyone some time to adjust," he added.

"No one should have to adjust to a murderer in the neighborhood," Cora snapped.

Dexter was tempted to remind her that, although some things shouldn't happen, it didn't mean that they would not.

TWENTY-TWO

MADISON'S FIRST THOUGHT on waking the next morning was that today was one day closer to Bates' release. She had to keep her determination to get strong, and after she had breakfast, she'd go for a walk to build her stamina. It was surprising how several days in the hospital had sapped her strength.

Usually she was so groggy from the lack of sleep that she couldn't eat until lunchtime, and then only a snack. But while she'd had a few moments of anxiety last night, the medication she'd taken must have put her immediately to sleep. Whatever the reason, the thought of her grandmother's Swedish pancakes, the special delicate crepe treats her grandmother made when Madison needed extra cheering, pushed thoughts of Bates aside.

But because she wanted Ella to rest today, she dug out the recipe card, gathered the ingredients, then put bacon on to fry.

"That smells wonderful, honey." Ella entered the kitchen and poured coffee. "But don't overdo today. You need to rebuild your strength."

Madison greeted her with a kiss, but couldn't help noticing that, although her grandmother had paid attention to her hair and clothes, she moved like an old woman. And an ill one.

She added a pat of butter to the sizzling skillet and poured the batter. Instantly, the scent of vanilla filled the kitchen.

"I'll do the cooking for the next couple of days. I'm not the only one who needs to rebuild strength," Madison said, turning the crepe.

Ella nibbled on a small bite of bacon. "I am tired," she admitted.

Now Madison was really alarmed. She couldn't ever remember her grandmother admitting to fatigue.

"More reason to let me pamper you a bit."

"But you're the one just out of the hospital."

"Look at all the rest I got. Now don't argue, Gran. I'm going to wait on you for a change."

When the first two pancakes were done, Ella pronounced them delicious and ate two bites before setting down her fork.

Madison piled three pancakes on her own plate. Her grandmother smiled.

"Glad to see you finally have an appetite. Greg's a good cook, isn't he?" Ella couldn't hide the twinkle in her eyes. "He's quite a catch, you know."

"Now don't start. I don't want to talk about him."

"He's a fine young man, and it would do you good to see him."

"I did see him last night."

"A date, dear. You know, those things where a young man and woman go to fun and exciting places and get to know each other. And on a regular basis."

"I'm not ready to see anyone on a regular basis," Maddy said, carefully wiping her mouth, "but I have decided to do something about my life. I'm going to start walking."

"Walking's good. But why the sudden interest?"

"Something happened in the hospital that I didn't tell you about. One time I woke and I was all alone in that room. You were in the bathroom, but I didn't know it. All I knew was that I was alone, hooked up to tubes, and all

I could think of was how helpless I'd be if Michael Bates walked into the room."

"Oh, honey, I'm so sorry."

"You have nothing to be sorry about. I'm glad it happened. It made me realize that I have to get myself in shape so I won't ever feel that helpless again. First thing is to build my stamina, and I can start by walking the hills behind your house like I used to do. And later today, I need to check my apartment and get my mail."

"Cora's been picking it up for you. It's on the buffet. She's a bit overwhelming at times, but her heart's good."

"Yeah, she is pretty overwhelming."

"Greg handled her pretty well. Shows he's sensitive to others and he can think on his feet. And don't forget, he's an excellent cook. All great qualities in a man, don't you think?"

"Gran, quit pushing it. If you keep it up, I'll recuperate at my apartment instead of here. Actually, it might be better that way. At least you'd get some rest."

"That's a terrible idea. I'd worry all the time. At least here I can see how you're doing. Promise you'll stay right here. Promise, Maddy."

Madison smiled. "I promise. But no more talk about Greg."

After clearing the dishes, Madison headed for her room, pulled on socks and her old Nikes, tied her hair into a ponytail, and dug her frayed red Disneyland ball cap from the closet.

"You're not going to overdo, are you?" Ella asked when Madison returned downstairs.

"I know my limits."

"Wear your boots, honey. It's the season for rattlers."

"You're always saying that, and I haven't seen one in years."

"Let's keep it that way."

Behind her grandmother's two-story home, several miles of brush-covered rolling hills climbed toward the San Bernardino Mountains, and Madison could see the rooftops of scattered homes nestled in the trees in the higher elevations.

Growing up, she'd always thought her grandparents' home was in a perfect location: separated just enough from the city to have the open feeling of country living, yet only minutes down the hill to Yucaipa.

About half a mile to the north, the Oak Glen Road led to the scenic apple-growing community at five-thousand feet, a place of apple orchards, family restaurants, and specialty shops. And less than four miles north from the Oak Glen Road, Highway 38, a two-lane winding road, climbed to Big Bear, a resort town sitting at seven-thousand feet.

On winter weekends, Madison's grandparents used to gather her, along with her friends, and take the winding road up for a day of snowboarding or skiing. And in the summer, they loved fishing at the lake. Now she simply took her grandmother into San Bernardino or to one of the casinos for an excellent Friday night seafood buffet.

Madison headed behind the house for her favorite childhood haunt, a hollow surrounded by trees a few hundred feet from Ella's back door.

Years ago, Dexter had helped her grandfather clear the brush and gather rocks for a circle of three fire pits, and Madison had joined them to scour the area for larger boulders to use as seats. Her grandfather said he'd rather she and her school friends spent their evenings in their personal campground than hot-rodding on the freeway.

Although she hadn't visited the area in several months, Madison still loved it. She brushed the dirt from her favorite white boulder that had a perfect dip in the middle, and sat, reminiscing about all the evenings spent with friends and dates around the campfire roasting hot dogs and making s'mores. Everyone told her how lucky she was to live in the hills. Most of them lived in Yucaipa or Calimesa in a normal neighborhood of residential streets lined with houses.

Her own parents had lived on a street like that, although, she'd realized later, a little more upscale, located in a subdivision close to Crafton Hills, a two-story brick home on a three-acre lot with a swimming pool. Sitting now on one of the dirty-white boulders, she thought about her former home, torn down about ten years ago because no one wanted to live in the house where two people had been brutally murdered.

Had her parents been wealthy? she wondered now. Was that why Bates had chosen her family? Her grandmother had never talked about family wealth or spoken as if they had money. Certainly her grandparents had never exhibited signs of wealth, and Madison couldn't remember feeling privileged as a child. Her parents had never lacked for necessities and even had some of the luxuries such as a nicer car, the latest TV, and had taken trips to Disneyland and the San Diego Zoo a couple of times a year, but her parents and grandparents had never acted like the rich people she'd seen on TV. Perhaps one day, if she could stand facing him, she'd ask Bates if he'd thought they'd had money in the house. Was that why he'd murdered her parents?

Birds chirping in the distance and squawking crows captured her attention, and she looked around, savoring the breeze rustling through leaves on the fir trees and the canyon live oaks. A clump of three aspens shaded her favorite boulder, and ponderosa pines stood as sentinels bordering the hollow. San Gorgonio peak, or Old Greyback as it's locally known, stood in the distance, its elevation of nearly twelve-thousand feet providing a bit of heaven right in Southern California.

Madison lifted her face to the puffy clouds. Was there such a place as heaven? If so, were her parents there now, watching over her as she used to believe? She had felt comforted in that belief, but now she didn't know.

But that uncertainty wasn't what haunted her. What alarmed her more than anything was that she had forgotten how her mother had looked. Madison could see her outline in her memory, but her mother's features were blurred. All she could distinctly remember was the sound of her mother's screams that night, the one thing she constantly prayed to forget.

Just thinking about them triggered the agonizing sound in her mind. She tried to think of something else, anything else, but the screams built in intensity just as they had that night. She covered her ears with both hands.

No! She didn't want to hear that sound!

She had to do something, anything, to push it from her mind, so she grabbed a slim aspen branch and swiped furiously at the ground leaves, sweeping them from the clearing, and when one branch snapped under her frenzy, she grabbed another and another.

But no amount of sweeping could erase the memory of that night. She relived it, waking to the horrible sounds, lying in bed terrified, every instinct urging her to run to her mother, yet the sounds of her screams so terrifying that Madison felt frozen to the bed—until sudden silence smothered the house, a silence so terrible that she forgot to breathe. She had lain listening intently to the unnatural sound until she heard the soft creeping footsteps in the hall, the sound her parents made when they wanted to check and make sure she was sleeping.

But that night, the footsteps were different, and they were creeping closer to her door.

What should she do? Pretend she was asleep? Her frantic pulse pushed her out of bed, and like a threatened animal, she ran to the only dark place to hide, the dark corner of her closet.

Panting, she peeked through the louvered slats. The door knob turned. She crouched down. He entered her bedroom, looked under the bed.

"Are we playing games?" He grinned, then raised the corners of her rumpled sheets.

She tried to hold her breath so he wouldn't hear her.

"I'm gonna find you," he chanted in a horrifying singsong voice. And with that evil grin, he looked directly at her through the closet door.

Now Madison swept the twig furiously around the boulders, fighting the memory and nausea that weakened her knees, jabbing in between to make sure no rattlers had nestled, hoping, praying she could forever erase that night like a bad movie on a videotape, when suddenly, her twig hit something solid.

Like a blessed miracle, her memories dissolved as she jabbed the twig again and again until it snapped. Whatever was between the two boulders was solid, so it wasn't a snake, a rabbit, or any other living creature. She grabbed a larger twig, crept closer, and jabbed harder to push the item, inch by inch, into the open.

When it emerged, she stared at a crumpled blood-splattered straw tote.